DISCARD

THE HONOUR OF THE BADGE

US Marshal Stewart Montague was a respected mentor to young Deputy Lincoln Hawk, guiding his first steps as a lawman and impressing upon him the importance of the honour of the badge. Twenty years later, the pair are pursuing a gang of bandits when Montague goes missing, presumed murdered. For six months, Hawk continues the mission alone, without success. But when he stumbles into the gang's hideout, there is a great shock in store. Seems his old companion isn't six feet under after all . . .

SCOTT CONNOR

THE HONOUR OF THE BADGE

Complete and Unabridged

LINFORD
Leicester

First published in Great Britain in 2013 by
Robert Hale Limited
London

First Linford Edition
published 2015
by arrangement with
Robert Hale Limited
London

A catalogue record for this book is available
from the British Library.

ISBN 978–1–4448–2570–1

Published by
F. A. Thorpe (Publishing)
Anstey, Leicestershire

Set by Words & Graphics Ltd.
Anstey, Leicestershire
Printed and bound in Great Britain by
T. J. International Ltd., Padstow, Cornwall

This book is printed on acid-free paper

Prologue

'Reach, lawman,' the outlaw demanded, his eyes streaks of ice.

Deputy Lincoln Hawk ignored the demand and stepped away until his back rested against the sheer rockface. The other two outlaws lay dead five paces to his left while his own six-shooter lay on the ground two paces to his right.

'You can still walk away from this,' Lincoln said, his voice calm, 'after a stretch in jail.'

'You can't have been a lawman for long if you reckon I'll listen to that.'

Lincoln shrugged, using the movement to draw attention away from his hand slipping behind his back to feel the rockface. He searched for a piece of rock he could break off to use as a missile once he'd distracted the outlaw, but the rock held firm.

'As you asked, this is my first assignment.'

'That's a tough break.'

The outlaw met his eye. Then he raised his gun a mite higher. A gunshot blasted.

Even though he knew the effort would be futile, Lincoln ducked down. He heard his heart thud, saw blood and a blur of movement. Then he was on his knees looking up and watching the outlaw collapse face first into the dirt.

Ten rapid heartbeats later, Lincoln was still feeling his chest with an unconscious action when US Marshal Stewart Montague stepped into view.

'That was a good ruse,' Stewart said breezily. 'Keeping him talking until I could sneak up on him.'

Lincoln hadn't thought Stewart was close enough to help him, but he nodded.

'I'm obliged you arrived when you did.'

Stewart looked him over, only his sly smile acknowledging he'd noticed Lincoln's worried tone and stiff posture.

'I'm impressed you worked out where they'd holed up. But tell me: what did it feel like facing death for the first time?'

Lincoln mustered a smile as he got to his feet and joined Stewart in checking the three outlaws were in fact dead.

'All I thought about was staying alive until I'd completed the mission, and ensuring he didn't get you too.' Lincoln rocked his head from side to side as he wondered what else he could learn from his first confrontation as a deputy marshal. 'And I knew that even if I failed, I'd get to die a lawman.'

'And now?'

'Pride, I guess.'

Stewart stood back from the dead men and slapped Lincoln heartily on the back, as if he'd provided the answer he wanted to hear.

'I assume that means you still want to be a marshal some day?'

'Some day, soon.'

'Then always remember how you felt here today. That's the honour of the badge.' Stewart tapped the star on his own chest. 'No matter how long you're a lawman and no matter where you go or what you do, never forget that.'

1

Twenty years later . . .

'A month chasing our own shadows,' Richmond Johnstone grumbled as he rode into East Town.

'And no sign of anyone else's,' Wallace Haycox said with a sigh. 'Unless we get some proper leads real quick, I'm not wasting any more of my time over this.'

Johnstone muttered that he agreed before he looked at US Marshal Lincoln Hawk for his reaction, but the marshal said nothing as he let his deputies work off their irritation.

A month ago Lincoln had deputized Johnstone and Haycox to help him track down Colm Tobin's gang of train-raiding bandits. They had carried out their duties diligently, so he didn't blame them for being irritated.

Lincoln himself was dreading making

his report to Moulton Casement, the railroad office boss, but when they dismounted outside the office, curiosity overcame his sombre demeanour.

Several men were inside and a lively debate was raging with much arm-waving and exasperated posturing, suggesting that while he had been away there had been developments.

'What's happened?' Lincoln demanded when he opened the door.

Silence descended and everyone in the room turned to him.

'This time it was a freight train, and it was carrying fifty thousand dollars,' Moulton said. He gestured at the other nine men in the room. 'These men have come from Alcove Springs, and it's gone, just gone.'

'If that much money's been stolen, then that sure means — '

'You don't understand,' Moulton shouted, cutting Lincoln off. 'It's not just the money. The train's gone too. Colm Tobin ordered everyone off the train, so they made their way back to

Alcove Springs afoot, but when they returned to the scene of the raid the train had gone. They continued down the tracks and it didn't reach East Town either.'

Lincoln's deputies both snorted and Lincoln gave Moulton an incredulous look, but everyone else in the room nodded.

'Colm Tobin,' Lincoln intoned, 'has stolen a train?'

Moulton set his hands on his hips and nodded sombrely.

'He sure did. The train has just vanished into thin air!'

* * *

The brakes were squealing like a banshee; that meant it was time for Lincoln to make his move.

He looked through the train window. Although he couldn't see the reason for this unscheduled stop five miles out of East Town, he caught the eyes of his deputies.

Both deputies leapt to their feet and followed him as he made his way down the aisle. He had reached the front when the train screeched to a shuddering halt, making him stumble into the door. Without breaking his stride, Lincoln threw open the door and took the right-hand side while his deputies went left.

When he peered beyond the engine he saw why the train had stopped. They had entered the narrow Stein's Pass and fifty yards beyond the cowcatcher at the midpoint of the pass stood a mound of rocks.

The sides of the pass were a stone's throw away and they were twice the height of the cars. On his side, the top was clear of movement and his deputies reported their side was clear too.

'Johnstone,' Lincoln said, 'keep the passengers inside. Haycox, scout around and see what we're facing.'

The deputies hurried away to do his bidding. Lincoln jumped down and walked beside the tracks. The engineers stayed in the engine; as he walked by one man shrugged while the other man looked around for trouble.

When he'd reached the cowcatcher, Haycox climbed up to the flat ground at the top of the pass. He shook his head, so Lincoln walked down the centre of the tracks to the mound of rocks and dirt, where he weighed up the possibilities.

Six months ago Colm Tobin's bandit gang had raided a passenger train fifty miles out of Alcove Springs. The bandits had deprived the passengers of their valuables.

When Colm mounted further attacks Lincoln and his old friend Marshal Stewart Montague had been tasked with bringing the bandits to justice, but Stewart had gone missing, presumed dead. Then a flood had swept away the Rocky Creek bridge, creating a break in the line and temporarily separating East Town from West Town, on either side of the creek.

It was several weeks before arrangements could be made to ferry passengers and cargo on the hundred-mile detour to rejoin the tracks. The activity appeared to curtail the bandits' raids but, with a larger and sturdier bridge nearing completion six miles downriver, last month the raids had restarted. So Lincoln had appointed two deputies.

After Colm had escalated his campaign and spirited away a train, Lincoln decided he had local knowledge and Moulton Casement agreed. Moulton suspected that one of the bandits was Quillon Dee, one of the influx of workers who were rebuilding the Rocky Creek bridge.

Lincoln had questioned Quillon, but he had dismissed Moulton's allegations while the overseer Philander Friedman had provided believable alibis to cover Quillon's whereabouts during the raids.

So, in seeking both to reassure passengers and solve the mystery of the vanishing train, Lincoln had headed to Alcove Springs and accompanied the next train to East Town. As it had turned out, on the way to Alcove Springs he had found no clues about the fate of the missing train, and on the way back, until encountering this rockslide, the journey had been trouble free.

Even then, the rockslide could be an unplanned calamity, as during the previous raids Colm had stopped the train with gunfire.

Now feeling confident that the landslide was natural, and irritated after yet another failure to advance his enquiry, Lincoln skirted around the mound. He was putting his mind to how they could clear the tracks when Haycox pointed down the pass.

'Lincoln,' he called, 'over there!'

Although Lincoln couldn't see what had concerned Haycox, he ducked down and sought cover behind the mound.

Deputy Johnstone heard the warning and hurried towards him. While Haycox dropped down from view, Johnstone joined him and the deputy wasted no time in pointing out a recess a hundred yards on from the mound.

'I saw movement over there,' Johnstone said. 'Three men came out and before they darted back into cover, they gestured to another man.'

Lincoln sighed. 'If this is a raid, it's not well organized.'

'The bandits keep changing their style.' Johnstone shrugged. 'Or perhaps they saw us and they panicked.'

Lincoln gave a supportive smile. 'Then let's give them even more reason to panic.'

Lincoln moved out from the mound and headed onwards with Johnstone at his right shoulder. They were twenty yards from the recess when Haycox fired, although he shot at a target that Lincoln couldn't see.

A moment later a man came into view, walking sideways uncertainly, with a hand clutched to a bloodied upper arm.

Haycox fired again. As his gunshot tore into the man's chest, Lincoln and Johnstone raised their guns.

They slammed quick shots around

the entrance to keep the other bandits down. While the shot man dropped to his knees and keeled over on to his side, Lincoln and Johnstone broke into a run.

As more of the recess became visible, Lincoln saw that it receded for fifty yards into the pass, its sides being sheer. He hunkered down at the entrance and with silent signals he directed Johnstone to cover him while he headed to the other side.

On the count of three he hurried off while he and Johnstone splayed wild covering gunfire about. Lincoln didn't see anyone other than the dead man, so when he'd covered the thirty paces to reach the safety of the other side he took a longer look.

The recess tapered to a point followed by an incline of loose rock, which could be climbed to reach the higher ground beyond, although the climb would be difficult.

The other men wouldn't have had time to escape, so when he'd reloaded he studied indentations in the rockface in which men could hide. Lincoln judged there wasn't enough space for many more people to be lurking here beyond those whom Johnstone had spotted.

He set off walking sideways with his back to the rock while on the other side, Johnstone matched his action. Ten paces on Johnstone stopped and looked at a point twenty paces on from Lincoln. Lincoln too stopped, a moment before a man darted out with a gun drawn.

'We don't mean no — ' the man shouted.

Lincoln shot him, cutting off his plea. The slug slammed into the man's side, making him drop to one knee to reveal that a second man had emerged. He'd already aimed his gun at Lincoln.

Two gunshots ripped out, the sounds echoing in the narrow recess like a drum roll. The trailing end of Lincoln's jacket flicked aside, but his own shot was more accurate and it clipped the man's cheek, making him grunt in pain as his hand rose to clutch his face.

The gun-toter doubled over while Johnstone caught him with a deadly shot through the top of his hat, which downed him. So Lincoln turned his gun back to the other man, but he stilled his fire when the man rolled on to his back, his gun falling from his grasp.

While Johnstone stayed put Lincoln hurried over to the wounded man and nudged him with his boot.

'How many more bandits are hiding out here?' he demanded.

'We're not . . . We weren't . . . ' the man murmured, his voice fading.

'If you'd thrown down your guns and surrendered, I'd have believed you didn't mean to ambush . . . ' Lincoln trailed off as the man exhaled a long gasping breath before lying still.

'That's the dangerous ones dealt with,' Johnstone shouted. 'We should give the rest one minute to throw down their guns before we finish them off.'

'That's too much time,' Lincoln shouted, also for the benefit of whoever was hiding in the recess. 'Give them ten seconds before we — '

'I've had enough!' an unseen man shouted. 'There's just me left and I'm not armed.'

'Then come out and I'll arrest you.' Lincoln waited but, getting no reply, he continued: 'I'm Marshal Lincoln Hawk and the other man's my deputy, Richmond Johnstone.'

When the deadline Lincoln had set passed without a reply, Johnstone moved on with his gun trained on the spot where they'd heard the man.

He didn't move quietly, so Lincoln wasn't surprised when their quarry made a bolt for freedom. He ran out from his hiding-place with his head down and hurried to the incline at the end of the recess.

The man was unarmed, so when Johnstone followed he didn't fire, but as he needed to be cautious in case others were hiding in the recess, he had covered only a dozen paces when the man reached the incline. The fugitive didn't get far.

He ran up the slope with his legs pounding, but the loose rocks absorbed his efforts and he soon came to a halt, after which he slid backwards until he toppled over. Then, flat on his chest, he slid down to ground level.

He shook off the failure and gained his feet, but this time he scrambled for only five paces before he lost his footing and slid backwards. He still tried again, but by then Johnstone had reached him.

The deputy slapped a firm hand on his collar and dragged him backwards. The man squirmed and continued trying to escape even when Johnstone pressed his gun up against his back.

As Lincoln was now sure this was the only man left for them to capture, he hurried on to help Johnstone.

'Quit struggling,' Johnstone said when Lincoln reached him. 'You're under arrest.'

'I'm not giving in,' the man bleated. 'I've done nothing wrong.'

Johnstone shot Lincoln an exasperated glance, but Lincoln took a moment to reply as he considered their prisoner's words. Then the man looked at him and the first sight of his small, shifty eyes, his weak jaw and his patchy beard made Lincoln snarl.

'You've done plenty wrong,' Lincoln muttered. 'The only reason I'm not shooting you where you stand is I want to see you swing.'

The prisoner made another attempt to break free, but that forced Johnstone to slap the back of his head with his gun, knocking him on to his chest. Then he knelt on his back to secure him before he looked at Lincoln.

'You know our prisoner?'

'Sure. He's Bernie Jacobson,' Lincoln sneered. 'He's a lawman-killer.'

2

Lincoln and his deputies stayed with the train to help the passengers clear away the landslide. This took an hour, and by the time the train trundled into East Town the passengers' delight at having been saved from a raid had died down.

Lincoln's own delight ended when Moulton Casement clambered into the car that Lincoln had commandeered to guard his prisoner and to house the bodies. Moulton identified the dead men as Safford Chance, Norwell Davis and Dugan McCloud.

'Six months of failure,' Moulton said, standing over the bodies, 'and then you kill ordinary working men from the bridge.'

Lincoln snorted in surprise. 'You suspected the bandits came from the bridge.'

'I did, but the bandits are ten masked men, all ruthless and all determined.' Moulton gestured at the bodies. 'These men aren't masked, and they're neither ruthless nor determined.'

'Even so, it doesn't change the fact that they were armed and lurking beside a landslide that stopped the train.' Lincoln raised a hand when Moulton started to object again. 'And they were holed up with this man, Bernie Jacobson, the killer of a US marshal.'

Bernie shook his head, as he had done whenever Lincoln mentioned his crime, and for the first time Moulton appeared lost for words.

'Bernie Jacobson killed a US marshal?' he spluttered when he found his voice, his eyes wide with surprise. 'That's nonsense. Bernie's so stupid that if he tried to kill a lawman he'd trip over his own feet, fall in a horse trough and drown.'

'Obliged for your support,' Bernie murmured. 'I think.'

'You wouldn't be so amused,' Lincoln muttered, 'if you'd known Marshal Montague. Any man who kills a lawman deserves to swing.'

'You're right about that.' Moulton walked up to Lincoln. 'I hope for your sake that you're right about the rest because I reckon you should have arrested Quillon Dee, not this wretch.'

'Philander Friedman vouched for Quillon.'

'Philander is scared of him. Quillon extorts wages from the workers, demands bribes, and anyone who stands up to him disappears, probably into the creek. He runs the bridge more than Philander does.'

Before Lincoln could retort, Moulton turned on his heel and jumped down from the car. While Moulton shouted out instructions for one of his assistants, Ambrose Taylor, to remove the bodies, Lincoln and his deputies followed him on to the platform.

Moulton's attitude having annoyed Lincoln, he let his deputies escort

Bernie to the railroad office. When they took Bernie inside, Lincoln stayed back to finger the badge he'd kept in his pocket for the last six months. Then he followed them inside.

Since the bridge had been swept away the town marshal, Uncas Yardley, had stationed himself in the larger West Town, leaving Moulton to dispense rudimentary authority from the railroad office.

While one of Moulton's workers, Ingram Watson, locked Bernie in a cell in the small jailhouse that had been erected behind the office, Lincoln drew his deputies aside to ask them for their opinions. They provided the ones he expected — and dreaded.

'We wanted those men to be bandits,' Johnstone said, 'so we could have our first success, but I reckon we got it wrong. They fought poorly and they were incompetent.'

'I agree,' Haycox said. 'Now I reckon they weren't lying in wait for the train. I was frustrated and if I hadn't got trigger-happy, they might not have fought back and we could have questioned them without bloodshed.'

Both men gnawed their bottom lips nervously, suggesting that they wanted Lincoln to prove them wrong. This was the first time they'd been called upon to act as lawmen and, despite his own misgivings, Lincoln had no trouble in complimenting them.

'You men did everything right,' he said. 'Even if Moulton's right and those men were decent workers, they were still acting suspiciously. Now make sure I'm not interrupted while I talk with Bernie.'

Lincoln nodded to his deputies, receiving smiles that were more assured than before. Then he headed into the jailhouse.

Bernie was the only prisoner, which clearly concerned Bernie as, when he saw Lincoln, he clambered up on to his cot and shuffled backwards into a corner of his cell.

'I've got nothing to say to you,'

Bernie said, anxiety making his voice high-pitched.

Lincoln didn't reply immediately, but took deep breaths to keep at bay the seething anger that had threatened to overcome him since he'd first seen Bernie.

'You had plenty to say to Marshal Montague,' he growled.

'Nobody knows what I said to him.' Bernie slid down to a sitting position where he drew his legs up to his chest and hugged them. 'That's why he paid me well.'

'He couldn't have paid you that well or you wouldn't have killed him.'

'I didn't kill him.'

Lincoln nodded while rubbing his jaw, as if he were digesting this information, then walked to the cell door. He paused before unlocking the door and swinging it open.

'In that case,' he said, forcing his lips to upturn with a grim smile, 'you can go.'

Bernie narrowed his eyes, clearly not

believing Lincoln's offer, but as Lincoln said nothing more, giving him no way to test it other than to leave, he slipped his feet down off the cot.

'Obliged,' he said cautiously.

Bernie found his hat, slapped it on his head and shrugged into his jacket. He even raised a foot on to the cot and buffed his boot as he delayed for as long as possible.

Throughout his making himself ready Lincoln maintained a thin smile, while fingering the badge in his pocket. Presently, with a worried gulp, Bernie moved for the door. Lincoln stepped back for a half-pace, encouraging Bernie to slip by.

The moment Bernie put a foot through the doorway, Lincoln grabbed his jacket and walked him back into the cell. He moved on until he slammed Bernie against the bars, then he dragged him forward only to slam him into the bars for a second time.

'I can now add trying to escape to your list of crimes,' he muttered.

'You've got nothing on me,' Bernie said as for the first time he gained enough confidence to smile. 'You released me so you could claim I escaped because that's the only crime you can charge me with.'

'You're a clever man to figure that out.' Lincoln waited until Bernie nodded, then he leaned forward to glare into his eyes. 'The only trouble is, Moulton reckons you're an idiot, which makes me think you've been lying and you were planning a raid in Stein's Pass.'

Bernie shrugged. 'The rail tracks will be connected to the new bridge next week, so we were patrolling the route when we came across the landslide. Before we could clear it, you shot us up.'

'The pass is five miles beyond the end of the tracks, so you couldn't have just come across the landslide, which means you were up to no good when a US marshal interrupted you.' Lincoln waited until Bernie rebutted the allegation with a grunt, then returned to the matter that most concerned him. 'Is

26

that what happened between you and Marshal Stewart Montague?'

'I was his informant until he stopped paying me. That's all I know.' Bernie raised his chin in defiance. 'I didn't even know he was dead until you claimed I'd killed him.'

Lincoln snarled with anger and slapped Bernie's cheek with a back-handed blow that sent him spinning away until he bumped into his cot. He folded over it, and when he tried to raise himself Lincoln leaned over him and shoved his face down into the mattress.

'If I were paying you for information,' he grunted, 'I'd demand a refund. Now tell me something I can believe.'

Lincoln raised Bernie's head from the mattress so he could reply, but, probably wisely, Bernie said nothing. So with the blood pounding in his ears Lincoln dragged Bernie upright and threw him across the cell.

Bernie slammed face first into the bars before his feet slipped from under him and he dropped to his knees. As he struggled to regain his feet, Lincoln moved in and grabbed the back of his head.

He tapped Bernie's forehead against the bars before dragging his head backwards so that Bernie looked up at him, his firm grip promising that the next time he knocked him against the bars he wouldn't be so gentle.

'Get off me,' Bernie whined. 'I don't know what happened to the marshal and I wasn't doing nothing wrong in Stein's Pass.'

'I didn't ask you about those incidents. I asked you to tell me something I can believe, or else this will happen.'

Lincoln rocked Bernie's head forward. At the last moment Bernie tried to turn his head to reduce the impact, but that attempt had the opposite effect as he left a clump of hair in Lincoln's hand and worse, he mashed his nose against a bar.

Blood dribbled down the bar as

Bernie bleated in pain and fell to the floor. He curled up while clutching his bleeding nose. Lincoln hunkered down beside him, waiting for him to stop complaining.

When Bernie showed he had overcome the pain by looking at him, Lincoln gave a wide smile that made Bernie shuffle away and then use the bars to drag himself up to a kneeling position.

'I'll tell you what happened,' Bernie said, speaking quickly and nasally. 'The marshal was looking for someone and I took him to see him. I never saw or heard of him again.'

Lincoln kept his expression stern. 'Name?'

'I won't tell you.' Bernie wiped blood from his upper lip and offered a tentative smile. 'Not without getting something in return.'

'Agreed. Tell me who you took Stewart to see and I won't smash your face into the bars again.'

Lincoln grabbed Bernie's collar and

stood up, dragging Bernie up on to tiptoes. Then he turned him round and jerked forward as if to complete his threat.

'Wait!' Bernie screeched. 'It was Quillon Dee. I took him to see Quillon Dee.'

Bernie had heard Moulton identify Quillon as a suspect and, as Bernie worked at the bridge, he would be familiar with Quillon's activities and know that he was a plausible culprit. Bernie tensed as he awaited Lincoln's verdict.

'I don't believe you,' Lincoln said.

Lincoln thudded a punch into Bernie's side, making him screech. Then he followed through with a backhanded blow that sent Bernie reeling into the corner.

'It's the truth,' Bernie blabbered, his hands raised before his face. 'I took him to see Quillon Dee. The marshal paid me and I left. Quillon's not a bandit, but he's a no-good varmint and he must have killed the marshal.'

'And today?'

'Today we were patrolling like I said when we . . . ' Bernie trailed off and sighed. When he resumed, his tone was low and for the first time honest-sounding. 'We found a body lying at the bottom of a ridge eight miles south of Stein's Pass. He was all broke up as if he'd fallen off the top, so we followed his tracks back to the pass. Then you arrived.'

Lincoln judged he'd heard some truth. He grabbed Bernie's shoulder, meaning to probe further as to which parts of this tale he could trust, but before he could speak Moulton Casement opened the jailhouse door.

'Leave him alone!' he demanded.

Lincoln glanced over his shoulder. 'I was just asking my prisoner a few questions.'

'Bernie is *my* prisoner.'

'You have no authority to take prisoners.'

'Marshal Yardley trusted me to look after East Town and on his behalf I say that until you can prove Bernie is a bandit, his only crime is acting suspiciously.'

'Given time, I'll prove it.'

'Either way, tomorrow I intend to conduct a proper search of the rail tracks back to Alcove Springs. While I'm gone you'll ask your questions from outside his cell.'

Lincoln was minded to argue, but Moulton's intervention had bolstered Bernie's confidence and he was smirking. Lincoln nodded to Bernie, promising that he hadn't finished with him yet. Then, without further comment, he left the jailhouse.

'Ingram fetched him,' Haycox said when Lincoln returned to the railroad office. 'We couldn't stop him bursting in.'

'It doesn't matter,' Lincoln said. 'I learnt plenty. Now we'll check out Bernie's story.'

Lincoln directed the deputies to join him in heading outside. With no further discussion they collected horses and rode out of town, taking the most direct route back to Stein's Pass.

Ambrose Taylor and five of Moulton's workers had arrived to clear away the last of the mound. They listened to Lincoln's report of events with stern expressions.

'Bernie and the other men were no bandits,' Ambrose said to supportive murmuring, 'and we haven't found anything to suggest the landslide wasn't natural.'

'Keep looking,' Lincoln said, 'and tell me if you find anything suspicious.'

Ambrose grunted, as if this were unlikely, but Lincoln still searched the recess. He found nothing untoward, so he followed up the other element of Bernie's story by heading south.

He soon found the body. It was as broken up as Bernie had described, while the clothes were compacted with dirt. The ridge was 300 feet high and the unfortunate man appeared to have fallen from the top and hit every obstacle on the way down.

The man had been dead for several

days, but his features had survived intact, which made Lincoln smile as the solution to several mysteries started to feel tantalizingly close. Without explaining his thinking, he directed his deputies to leave the body where it was and join him in moving on to Rocky Creek.

The bridge had become within view when Haycox asked the question that Lincoln had been expecting.

'Did you know Marshal Stewart Montague well?'

'I did. More years ago than I care to recall he deputized me for a special assignment. It would have been a short assignment if he hadn't saved my life. Later, when I became a US marshal, he remained a good friend.'

'What happened to him?'

'When we joined forces to track down Colm Tobin, we got different leads. We separated. I never saw him again.'

'What made you think Bernie killed him?'

'Stewart's lead *was* Bernie. I followed their trail, but I found only this.' Lincoln removed Montague's badge from his pocket and held it up. 'Bernie says Stewart met Quillon Dee.'

'So you reckon Quillon's a bandit?'

'No.' Lincoln pointed back at the ridge. 'But the dead man back there was. That was Colm Tobin, our bandit leader, which means we're on the verge of ending his gang's reign of terror.'

Johnstone only shrugged, but Haycox joined Lincoln in whooping with delight before the lawmen speeded to a trot. As it turned out, Lincoln's good mood lasted only until he saw the reception committee awaiting them at the bridge.

Work had stopped and around fifty men had congregated by the bodies of the three men who had been killed in the pass. When one of the workers saw them, a ripple of consternation spread through the crowd until everyone turned to face them.

'Stand tall and do your duty,' Lincoln

35

said when his deputies looked at him for guidance. 'We did nothing wrong and we have nothing to fear.'

'I know,' Haycox murmured, 'but I doubt they'll accept that.'

When the men on the outskirts of the crowd peeled away to collect tools and waved their makeshift cudgels above their heads, Lincoln had to agree.

3

'You killed my workers,' Philander Friedman accused when Lincoln drew up before him.

'They confronted lawmen and they died,' Lincoln said. He dismounted and walked on to meet Philander, even though that encouraged the crowd on either side to edge closer. 'Now explain what they were doing in Stein's Pass.'

'I don't know, but they were conscientious workers: when they saw trouble they'd have tried to deal with it. Either way, they weren't bandits. I can vouch for them all.'

'Like you vouched for Quillon Dee?' When Philander gulped and nervously rubbed his brow, Lincoln pointed at him. 'I now know Quillon was involved in a lawman's murder. So where is he?'

Philander shook away his surprise and in return he pointed a truculent finger at Lincoln.

'First, you claimed my workers are bandits and now you claim they killed a lawman. I reckon after six months of Colm Tobin running rings around you, you took out your frustration on innocent men. Now you're desperate to prove something to justify killing them.'

'Colm won't run rings round nobody no more,' Lincoln said as Philander's valid comment caused consternation around them, 'and they weren't innocent.'

The workers edged closer while the men standing behind Lincoln closed ranks to create a circle with him at the centre. As the mob's anger rose, one man stepped forward and hurled a pick-axe handle.

Lincoln ducked and the handle spun ineffectually over his head before crashing into the workers on the other side. A worker fell over clutching a bruised knee, which only added to the men's anger. Another man picked up the handle and threw it back.

His aim was worse than the first man's aim had been and the handle flew over the heads of the circle of workers. As it disappeared from view, the man shouted a defiant oath. As if that was the rallying cry everyone had been waiting for, the circle closed in on Lincoln and his deputies.

Most of the men were armed with cudgels, the rest had fists raised and bloodlust in their eyes. Lincoln glared at the nearest men, aiming to show no fear and force them to back down, but their hunched postures and stern-set expressions said they were beyond reasoning with.

Then they charged and, within moments, they overwhelmed Lincoln.

He batted the first man to reach him aside with the flat of his hand. He grabbed the second man's shoulders and hurled him into the path of the nearest two attackers, sending all three men tumbling.

He thumped the next man in the stomach before delivering an uppercut that toppled him backwards, but the men behind him were moving purposefully. The falling man didn't halt them for even a moment; they pressed in tightly on all sides.

Lincoln whirled his fists, hammering blows into the faces that came within reach and for a while he held his position, but then someone hit him from behind with a cudgel. His vision darkened and he stumbled forward towards men who greeted him with solid punches that knocked him backwards.

Before he could regain his senses two men grabbed his arms from behind and he was held rigid. Space opened up as the mob spread out to give a burly man enough space to pummel him.

When that man stepped forward with his eyes lively and his fists raised, Lincoln struggled. He dragged an arm free, but then a gunshot rattled.

The blast instilled calm as everyone froze, and Lincoln used what could be a temporary hiatus to free his other arm.

He shoved his assailants aside before he drew his own gun.

He saw that Moulton Casement had arrived with Ambrose Taylor and Ingram Watson. Moulton had fired, while Ambrose and Ingram were holding their guns aimed high. Lincoln joined Moulton in firing into the air.

'That shot was for the clouds,' Lincoln shouted. 'Tell me where Quillon Dee is, or I start making arrests.'

His demand made Philander laugh and look around as he sized up the overwhelming forces aligned against the lawmen. The hilarity at least stopped anyone from acting.

'Even with Moulton,' Philander declared, 'you're outnumbered by eight to one. You're in no position to make demands.'

Lincoln tapped his star. 'This says I'm the only one who can make demands.'

Lincoln and Philander considered each other. Philander was the first to look away.

'Quillon headed into East Town,' Philander said, his voice low.

'Obliged for the information. I'll have more questions for you later.'

'This time I co-operated.' Philander glanced at the three bodies. 'But if you come here again with accusations and no proof, I won't be so understanding.'

Haycox and Johnstone were getting to their feet, and Lincoln gestured to his deputies to leave. Together they turned on their heels and made their slow way through the gap that was forming as the workers peeled away.

'You reckon they'll come after us?' Haycox asked, eyeing the surrounding men with concern.

'Only if they have something to hide,' Lincoln said, 'which means it's likely.'

Haycox nodded, but Johnstone said nothing. Both men looked at him. When he registered that they were interested in him, Johnstone took a deep breath before replying:

'Philander was right,' he said. 'Quillon's a no-good varmint, but the dead men weren't. You're looking for conspiracies to cover up the fact that we killed three innocent men.'

Neither Lincoln nor Haycox replied and the three men moved away, covering all the directions from which someone might attack them. But the workers didn't pursue them, and when they reached clear space, Moulton considered the disgruntled mob, his upper lip curled with wry amusement, before he paced up to them.

'So,' Lincoln said, 'you've finally decided to act, have you?'

'I have,' Moulton said. 'I talked to Bernie Jacobson and he told me what happened in Stein's Pass. So I'm taking Deputy Haycox prisoner pending a proper investigation from Marshal Yardley in West Town.'

Haycox jerked upright with shock before stepping forward with words of complaint on his lips, but Lincoln slapped an arm across his chest, halting him.

'My deputy followed my orders.'

'Bernie said Haycox fired first without provocation and before you gave any orders.' Moulton stepped to the side to face Haycox. 'So come quietly and we'll deal with this in a proper, lawful manner.'

Haycox looked at Lincoln for direction. Lincoln shook his head.

'He's going nowhere,' he said, moving between Moulton and Haycox. 'He's my deputy and I take responsibility for his actions.'

While Moulton and Lincoln faced each other, Ambrose and Ingram stepped up to stand beside Moulton. When neither man looked like backing down, Haycox stood at Lincoln's left shoulder, encouraging Johnstone to close ranks, but the effect was lost when Johnstone barged into Lincoln.

Moulton's eyes opened wide with surprise, alerting Lincoln to a problem a moment before Johnstone jabbed a gun into his ribs.

'Nobody's following your orders no more,' Johnstone muttered.

Lincoln glanced at Johnstone and snarled when he saw that when the deputy had barged into him he had wrested his Peacemaker from its holster.

'You've just made the worst choice of your life,' Lincoln said.

'I reckon I've made my first right choice since you deputized me.'

Lincoln didn't reply, and Haycox had no choice but to join Moulton. He turned to face his former fellow deputy and rolled his shoulders.

'If Lincoln doesn't get to you,' he muttered, 'you'll have to deal with me.'

Moulton directed Ambrose and Ingram to secure Haycox, but Haycox waved his arms while barging past them, signifying he didn't need escorting. Moulton accepted his attitude with a sly smile and followed.

'Comply with Moulton's orders,' Lincoln shouted after Haycox, 'and as soon as I can I'll get you out of the jailhouse.'

'You won't do nothing,' Moulton said as he mounted up, 'other than join him in a cell.'

Lincoln resisted the urge to retort; instead he addressed Johnstone.

'What do you plan to do now?' he asked.

'I'll see if Philander will employ me. At least then I can hold my head up high.'

Lincoln watched Moulton and the others leave. When this made Johnstone look at them, Lincoln swept an arm backwards, catching Johnstone's wrist and slapping the gun aside.

He twisted round and with his other hand, he grabbed Johnstone's elbow before driving on and toppling him. Johnstone landed on his chest with his arms splayed. Before he could fight back Lincoln knelt on his chest and wrested the gun from his outstretched hand.

'You got that wrong,' Lincoln muttered, jabbing the gun into Johnstone's side. 'We're both heading back to town. I'll speak for Haycox and I'll speak against you.'

Johnstone raised his head and snorted

a laugh with surprising confidence. A moment later Lincoln saw what had given him heart.

Moulton having left the bridge, the workers had taken a renewed interest in the marshal and they were closing in with determined paces. Lincoln aimed at the nearest man, which made him stop and slip back into the crowd, but another man took his place, proving that they hoped their superior numbers would prevail.

Then pounding footfalls sounded behind him as several men moved in quickly. Before Lincoln could turn, he was bundled over and knocked away from Johnstone.

Within moments he was disarmed. Two men secured his arms and another two grabbed his legs.

To his relief, the mob didn't seek to exact immediate retribution. He was raised from the ground and carried towards the bridge. He was brought to stand upright before Philander, who considered developments with his arms folded.

A swarthy, brooding hulk of a man stood at Philander's shoulder, making Lincoln narrow his eyes.

'Quillon Dee's returned,' Philander said, 'and he's not pleased about your activities.'

Despite his captors' firm grips, Lincoln glared at Quillon.

'You're under arrest, Quillon,' he declared, 'for the murder of US Marshal Stewart Montague.'

'Defiant words,' Quillon said.

Quillon gestured and a sack was drawn down over Lincoln's head by a man who had been standing behind him. Then, as Quillon laughed, he was clubbed on the back of the head with a fierce blow that knocked him to his knees.

4

With his head trapped inside the sack Lincoln was dragged forward and thrown to the ground at the top of the river-bank.

He was pinned down while Philander and Quillon talked. Their hushed tones suggested that his fate was being discussed. Lincoln couldn't hear their words, but Philander was calm and Quillon spoke with urgency.

Quillon appeared to win the debate as he spoke last and then moved over to stand before Lincoln.

'Any man who helps you,' Lincoln said, 'is as guilty as you are.'

'What makes you think I mean you harm?'

Quillon's tone was tense, so Lincoln responded appropriately.

'Because you haven't answered my questions yet about Marshal Montague.'

'I'll answer any questions. I have nothing to hide and I mean you no harm, despite what you did to these men.'

'This is a dangerous game, Quillon,' Philander called, his tone sounding disgusted. 'I want no part of it.'

As Philander moved away on to the bridge, a dragging noise sounded as something was placed before Lincoln. He was drawn up to his feet and shoved forward.

After taking two steps, he bellied up to an object that creaked when it moved. Acrid whiskey fumes drifted beneath the sack, telling Lincoln he was standing before a barrel.

He backed away, forcing his captors to grab his legs and lift him inside. Then, with his captors holding his hands behind his back, they tried to shove him to his knees, but the barrel was large and Lincoln was able to spread his legs wide apart and brace himself.

For a minute Lincoln fought back,

resisting the attempt to push him down. Then more men approached. More than five pairs of hands pressed on his back and shoulders while other men shouted encouragement.

The moment he dropped to one knee, he was released and the lid was slapped down against his back. The lid thudded into place, giving Lincoln the impression that someone had sat on it. Lincoln used his freedom to tear the sack from his head.

Darkness greeted him. While he could hear men moving around outside he pushed the lid experimentally, but found it set firmly in place.

Then hammering sounded as his captors nailed the lid down. Lincoln flexed his arms and rolled his shoulders as he relaxed his muscles in preparation for fighting back.

He didn't ask what Quillon's intentions were, figuring that he'd find out soon enough and it was unlikely to be welcome. Sure enough, the barrel rocked before it was tilted to the side.

Then the barrel was rolled on its edge and Lincoln struggled to keep his balance, but it was moved for only a few yards. Shuffling sounded as someone settled down before he tapped on the wood to get Lincoln's attention.

'Do you want to explain,' Quillon said, speaking a few inches away from Lincoln's right ear, 'what you did in the pass?'

'You're the only man who'll explain anything,' Lincoln said. 'You'll start by telling me why you killed Marshal Montague, you'll move on to revealing the location of the missing train, and you'll end by explaining why you've taken a lawman prisoner.'

'I didn't kill the marshal, I don't know where the train went, and nobody is keeping you prisoner.'

Quillon laughed, and when that encouraged other men to laugh, Lincoln sought a gap in the wood so he could see how Quillon was amusing them.

He couldn't find any gaps; worse, his movement rocked the barrel, generating more laughter and giving Lincoln a precarious feeling. This turned out to be warranted when the barrel tipped over.

He fell head over heels and continued to tip forward until the base was beneath him again. Roars of laughter peeled out, the sound becoming fainter as if the men were now some distance away letting Lincoln guess what had happened.

As the riverbank was the only place the barrel could roll down, he presumed Quillon had positioned him precariously at the top. When Lincoln had moved, his actions had toppled the barrel, which presumably would let Quillon claim he had only meant to frighten Lincoln and he hadn't intended for him to end up in the creek.

This was no comfort to Lincoln, who continued rolling as the barrel gained speed down the bank. As he fought to orient himself, he recalled that the creek was high and about fifty feet below the bridge, but before he could remember other details, his forehead clattered against the side, making him go limp.

He rolled around inside the barrel, which turned out to be the best way to deal with the situation, as the curved sides let him move with ease.

A thud sounded and Lincoln had a momentary feeling of being airborne before another thud jarred him, after which he began rocking back and forth.

Lincoln was struggling to fight off the effects of his earlier blow; only when his left hand became damp did he realize that the barrel had rolled into the creek and water was leaking in. The current buffeted him, but the barrel had settled upright, enabling Lincoln to kneel.

He sought out the leak, finding that moisture was seeping in around the lid. He tried to plug the gap with his hands, but he couldn't keep his hands still while rocking.

Then the barrel shifted position, forcing Lincoln to lean against the side. Worse, water poured in with greater speed, drenching him within moments, although the cold water revived his senses.

After a minute water sloshed around

his ankles. Lincoln removed his jacket and pressed it against the rim. For several minutes the water stopped seeping inside, but before long, his jacket became soaked and the water rose up above his knees.

He put his jacket on again and, when the barrel bucked and made him slide around, he decided that trying to stay the water's progress was only delaying the inevitable. He had to escape before the barrel filled with water and sank.

While the barrel swirled as if it had been caught in an eddy, he stayed his movement by bracing his back against the curved side. Then he drew his legs up to brace them against the other side and shoved the lid with an outstretched hand.

That action didn't move the lid and it only made him slide away towards the base along the slippery inside. He took up a more secure position by jamming his back and shoulders against the base and planting his feet on the lid.

He pressed his hands against the

sides to keep himself steady. That made him suffer an odd feeling of moving rapidly, even though he seemed not to be actually moving. As nausea made him giddy, he kicked out and succeeded at last in making the lid spin away.

He enjoyed a brief moment of elation as light flooded in. The elation quenched when water followed the light, slapping him in the face with all the ferocity of a double-handed punch.

Lying in an awkward position, he couldn't stop the water filling his mouth, making him choke and splutter. It took him several attempts to right himself and by then water filled the inside. Even more troubling, the light level had dropped.

He willed himself to stop panicking and take stock of the situation. That let him confirm that the water-laden barrel was sinking into the creek's impenetrable depths.

Buzzing filled his ears, loud enough to drown out the roaring water, and his lungs tightened, demanding air. He kicked out and, with a scrambling motion that knocked his knees and elbows against the sides of the barrel, he clawed his way out through the top.

He emerged in an ungainly fashion with his arms and legs waving, and tried to swim away, but he had to struggle to get clear. Then the barrel tipped over and caught him a stinging blow to the jaw.

His mouth opened, expelling the last of his air. In desperation he swam away from the barrel, which within moments disappeared from view into the swirling, murky water.

He reckoned he was making progress and he would reach the surface with a few more strokes, but then in a disorientating moment he noticed it was lighter in the direction he thought was below him.

With a groan he accepted that he was swimming towards the creek bottom. In the strong current he fought to turn, but when he faced the surface that direction was dark too and the pressure on his lungs no longer felt troubling.

He stopped struggling.

Damp ground was beneath Lincoln's chest and a chill wind bit through his wet clothing.

After his troubling time in the barrel these feelings were strangely refreshing and he enjoyed stretching out, but soon the coldness made him shiver. He rolled over on to his back to find it was dark.

The creek didn't sound as loud as it had before, and he thought he heard voices. While he'd been in the barrel he must have drifted downstream for some distance and so he assumed he'd been mistaken about the voices.

He sat up and slapped the side of his head to free water from his ears; the movement made his stomach lurch. He fought down the feeling of nausea with deep breaths, but because he'd swallowed so much creek water the air he wheezed in and out tasted foul.

He leaned over and retched. When he'd coughed up a bellyful of water, a wave of euphoria at having survived made him light-headed. With a spring in his step, he got to his feet.

When his eyes became accustomed to the low light, he examined his surroundings and confirmed he'd washed up in an area where high rocks were on three sides. He could see that out on the water the current was placid.

He could still hear voices and he noticed that a light source was reflected near by. The flickering confirmed it was a fire.

He sloshed through the mud away from the creek until he saw the fire at the base of the rockface. Although he'd prefer to isolate himself, his wet clothing was plastered to his skin and the starry sky promised that the night would get only colder.

He wasn't armed and when he felt his chest he realized that he'd lost his badge. With his teeth chattering, he walked briskly to generate warmth, but he failed.

By the time he reached dry ground he was walking stiff-legged and the joy he'd felt from having survived had died out. Whether the people who had taken refuge in this area welcomed his arrival or not, he had to reach the warmth of the fire.

He faced the reflected light and moved on. After a few paces, undergrowth blocked his path. He batted branches aside until his strength gave out, after which only his momentum drove him on.

The chatter grew louder, its cheerful nature giving Lincoln hope. When he broke free of the undergrowth he saw that the fire was twenty feet ahead. Rudimentary tents had been pitched before the rockface and five men were sitting around the fire.

Daniel Tobin, the younger brother of the former bandit leader, was looking at him, after presumably hearing his progress through the undergrowth, and he leapt to his feet. Then, while shouting a warning to the others, he hurried towards Lincoln.

Lincoln realized with a groan that

he'd washed up in the bandit gang's hideout. Daniel grabbed Lincoln's shoulders and drew him forward. Lincoln was too weak to protest, and when he was thrown to the ground his only response was to crawl towards the heat.

He was starting to enjoy the warmth when another man whom he recognized from a Wanted poster as Kimball Sutherland slapped a hand on Lincoln's back and dragged him to his feet.

'Who are you?' Kimball demanded. When Lincoln didn't reply but simply stood hunched over, he continued: 'What are you doing here? How did you find us?'

Lincoln's senses were still too befuddled after his ordeal for him to work out how he should respond, so he remained silent. With an exasperated grunt Kimball shoved him away, sending Lincoln reeling into Daniel, who shoved him back.

This time Lincoln stumbled to his knees, where with his head lowered so that his chin rested on his chest, he swayed while fighting to stay upright. A murmured debate started, but Lincoln struggled to concentrate on it.

The debate ended when a new man came out of a tent. He moved over to Lincoln and walked around him.

As the man said nothing Lincoln put a hand to the ground and shoved himself to his feet. He stumbled before he planted his feet wide apart and then raised his head to face the newcomer, a man with a trim greying beard and stern eyes.

To his surprise, this man was his old friend Marshal Stewart Montague, who considered him with his eyebrows raised in bemusement.

'I . . . I . . . ' Lincoln murmured, struggling for words.

He didn't get enough time to complete his statement before Stewart stepped up to him and offered a tense smile. Then Stewart delivered a swinging punch to his jaw that sent Lincoln spinning to the ground.

5

Lincoln was too weak to fight back. Kimball and Daniel grabbed his arms and dragged him away from the fire.

They deposited him inside a tent, after which they left. Presently Stewart came inside.

'I thought you were dead,' Lincoln murmured.

'Men like us never give up,' Stewart said, hunkering down beside him. 'It's good to see you again.'

'And you.' Lincoln rubbed his jaw ruefully. 'So why did you hit me?'

Stewart glanced outside before lowering his voice.

'I had to stop you blurting out your name and status.' He waggled a warning finger. 'Tell nobody who you are other than what I've told everyone: that you're an old friend.'

Lincoln grunted, receiving a quick

nod from Stewart. Then he sat up. When he noted that even thirty feet away from the fire the heat still warmed him he squeezed out the dampness from his clothes.

'So I guess you're working under cover, and you started by throwing Colm Tobin off . . . ' Lincoln fell silent when Stewart raised a cautionary hand. 'I'll leave my questions, provided I can have food and heat and sleep.'

'I'll fetch you something to eat.' Stewart patted his shoulder before moving away. 'Just stay here and avoid everyone as much as you can.'

Lincoln didn't need any further encouragement to lie down, although he couldn't relax, as Stewart was sure to need his help soon. So he watched him gather food and interact with the bandits, while trying to understand the group's dynamics.

Needing to avoid looking suspicious, Lincoln didn't watch too studiously and it was hard to work out who was the new leader. In fact, the men often looked to Stewart for instructions.

When Stewart returned with water, hard bread and even harder cheese, along with a towel and a blanket, Lincoln said nothing. He concentrated on getting warm and eating, leaving the questions until a safer time.

Stewart watched him with a smile on his lips, enjoying being reunited with his old friend. Once Lincoln had dried out the companionable silence made him yawn and he didn't resist when his eyelids drooped.

He fell into a deep sleep during which the night passed without him waking. Only movement in the camp in the morning woke him. Stewart wasn't in the tent, and Lincoln lay where he could watch anyone who strayed close.

The morning light showed that the bandits had chosen their hideout well. The rocks around their haven looked even steeper than they had done last night, being 400 feet high and over-hanging in places.

The hideout was a hundred paces

across and the fact that he couldn't see horses but could see a moored boat suggested the only access was by water. If this was where the bandits holed up between raids, he could see how they'd remained undetected.

This observation added to Lincoln's curiosity about how Stewart had infiltrated the group. After a night's sleep, he could think more clearly, letting him recall how Stewart had operated in the past.

'What's happening here?' Lincoln asked when Stewart returned.

'I told you,' Stewart said with a glance outside to check that nobody was close, 'we have to keep quiet.'

'But you've never worked like this before,' Lincoln whispered. He removed Stewart's badge from his pocket. Since finding it six months ago he had never thought he would have the chance to present it to his old friend. 'When you wore this, the law was clear. Undermining outlaws wasn't your way.'

'It wasn't, but don't mention this

again. This place is small. We can't risk being overheard.' Stewart pointed at the badge. 'And put that away before it gets us both killed.'

'If we're discovered, we'll deal with it together.' Lincoln waited until Stewart nodded before he slipped the badge back in his pocket. 'I met an old friend, Quillon Dee, at Rocky Creek.'

Stewart tensed before he smiled, confirming they could exchange information by talking subtly, although when he replied he spoke quietly.

'I met him six months ago. I'm sorry I didn't wait to explain, but I had to act quickly when I learnt Colm was planning something big.'

Stewart gestured upriver, presumably signifying the railroad.

Lincoln snorted a rueful laugh. 'And it doesn't get much bigger than stealing a train.'

Stewart clamped his lips closed and conveyed with flared eyes that Lincoln should be less direct. Then he flinched and leapt to his feet.

'I'll deal with it, Daniel,' Stewart said, raising his voice.

Stewart shot Lincoln a warning glare and then slipped out of the tent. A moment later Daniel Tobin approached.

Without acknowledging Lincoln again, Stewart and Daniel headed away. They glanced his way frequently, showing they were discussing him and the debate concluded with both men walking towards the creek.

Other men joined them until everyone was heading to the water. Figuring that staying in the tent when everyone was being active would look suspicious, Lincoln went outside.

He followed the bandits, confirming they were going to the boat. Kimball, a man who appeared eager to please, reached the water first.

Kimball shoved the boat into the water and steadied it to let the others clamber aboard. When the men lined up with Stewart at the rear, Lincoln stopped at the edge of the undergrowth.

Stewart must have been aware that

this development would concern him as when everyone but he had boarded the boat, he bade them wait and made his way up from the water.

'Where are you going?' Lincoln said, speaking loudly so that everyone could hear.

'That's not your concern,' Stewart said, not meeting his eye. 'While we're gone, guard the camp and that'll repay your debt to me. When we return, you can leave.'

Clearly Stewart had told a story to explain his presence, but Lincoln's distaste at seeing his old mentor working with these men made him uneasy. He couldn't bring himself to care if the bandits became suspicious of him and he ruined Stewart's scheme to undermine them.

'What's your plan?' he said quietly.

Stewart met his eye, his expression horrified and, as the question had been a neutral one, the fact that he'd spoken quietly must have concerned him.

'Say nothing more,' Stewart said with

quiet urgency, 'or you'll ruin everything.'

'One of my deputies turned on me while the other followed my orders and got arrested. I have to resolve that as well as helping you. I can't do that if I stay here.'

Stewart had raised a hand, but when it failed to still Lincoln's litany of concerns, he limited himself to narrowing his eyes.

'I'm leaving now,' he said with stern finality.

'You're leaving with bandits.' Lincoln glanced at the men in the boat, who were watching their discussion eagerly. 'They're a motley bunch of no-account varmints who treat you with so much respect, it's as if you've become their new leader.'

Stewart opened his mouth to retort, but then, presumably after taking offence at Lincoln's jibe, without comment he turned on his heel.

That only increased Lincoln's annoyance. He moved forward and his squelching footfalls encouraged Stewart to swirl round, his fists clenched and his expression as tense as it had been last night when he'd hit him.

Lincoln clenched his fists and the two old friends faced each other. Lincoln was sure their confrontation would end in them trading blows, but perhaps because his old friend had seen the intent in his eyes, with a sigh, Stewart backed away.

Lincoln slipped a hand in his pocket, reminding Stewart of the badge he still carried and that made Stewart firm his jaw before he turned swiftly. He hurried down to the creek where Kimball helped him to climb into the packed boat.

When everyone was in position the bandits glared up at Lincoln with apparent distrust. Lincoln didn't react other than to move down to the shallows, where he watched Stewart chat with the men.

Daniel took up oars and directed the boat away, which took everyone's attention away from Lincoln. As the boat slipped through the water, jovial chatter started up.

Just before the boat drifted out of view beyond the downriver headland, Kimball slapped Stewart's back and laughed. Stewart never looked at Lincoln.

For fifteen minutes after the boat had disappeared from view, Lincoln stared at the headland. He couldn't decide which part of the morning's events disturbed him the most. He returned to the camp.

Even if he didn't agree with what Stewart was doing, he still trusted that he had a plan to bring the remaining bandits to justice. As he'd been left here alone, he searched the camp for evidence of their activities.

He found only a small amount of food, discarded clothing and playing cards, suggesting their departure had been planned, so he looked for a way out. He started at the creek and studied the sheer wall.

He could see no way to reach the top, so he walked around the perimeter. Above were rocks and scrawny vegetation that presented handholds and footing, but when he fingered some ledges they broke off and he doubted whether any of them were strong enough to support his weight.

When he reached the back of the area, he found a section where running water had exploited a crack in the rock. It had created a narrow gully filled with loose stones and with a shallower incline than elsewhere.

If he were lucky, he might be able to clamber up this gully, but even so, one wrong move and he would tumble back down to the ground. Worse, his growing understanding of the location helped him to work out that he was looking at the other side of the ridge from where Colm Tobin had fallen to his death.

Colm's fate suggested that clambering around up there when he didn't know the area could be foolhardy; he should risk trying this route only as a last resort.

So he walked around the back of the camp and on to the water's edge. This side proved to be as steep as the other side was. Disheartened, Lincoln slumped down on a boulder.

He contemplated the headlands to either side. He judged there weren't enough handholds and ledges to let him climb around either of them. As a last resort he considered the creek.

The water beyond the headland was roiling and brown, but he had survived his journey from the bridge. Provided he could get back on to dry land shortly after rounding the headland, this was his best escape route.

He moved to the rockface. He was staring at the downriver headland, trying to judge what was in the area he couldn't see, when unexpected movement came.

Daniel and Kimball were returning in the boat and, as they were moving upriver, they were both rowing.

Lincoln's guarded conversations with Stewart hadn't suggested these men would return quickly and he moved away from the creek. His movement caught Kimball's attention and, as they entered calmer water where only one man needed to row, he put down his oars.

Maintaining his cover of being Stewart's friend, Lincoln saluted him. Kimball returned the gesture but, unfortunately, clutched in his raised hand was a six-shooter.

He fired and the shot clattered into the rock a foot from Lincoln's leg. This encouraged Daniel to turn in the boat and raise his own gun.

Lincoln didn't need any further warnings. He dived into the under-growth as two gunshots whistled above his tumbling form. He scrambled into hiding, then looked around the site, but as he'd realized earlier, there was no easy way out.

6

Daniel and Kimball clambered out of the boat. Thankfully, they were confident and so they acted slowly as they enjoyed the situation.

Lincoln vowed to make them pay for their over-confidence, and when he emerged from the undergrowth he hurried to the camp. Earlier he'd failed to find anything incriminating, but now he'd settle for finding something he could use as a weapon.

He rummaged through discarded clothing, but the bandits had left only soft items and by the time he'd searched the camp he'd gathered only several branches that had been brought in for firewood.

By now Kimball and Daniel were batting the undergrowth aside, so he rolled up the canvas tent in which he'd slept last night. Then, with the tent tucked under an arm and three short branches clutched to his chest, he hurried to the back of the site.

This area was exposed and the only place where he could hide was the gully that he'd dismissed as a possible escape route. If he headed in there he would be trapped, but it was also a position he could defend.

He slipped into the gully. After ten paces he climbed up the slope. Then, after another ten paces, he turned a corner and moved out of view from the site.

The rocks underfoot were small and loose. So every step was hard fought and the route was cramped.

Standing in the middle of the gully, he could touch both sides with his outstretched hands. Higher up the slope became steeper while the rocks were lodged even more precariously.

He figured that if he continued climbing his escape would be no more successful than Bernie's had been in Stein's Pass. He decided the best position to hide out was just beyond the corner.

He sat down with his back against the rockface. As he listened to his pursuers' progress, he dumped the canvas tent and branches down beside him. Kimball and Daniel were reporting to each other about their search, using loud and irritated tones.

Before long they would work out that he was here, so Lincoln flattened the tent while considering defensive strategies. Without a plan in mind he collected rocks and placed them on the tent.

He bunched up the canvas and hefted it, creating a heavy sack. He reckoned that if he could lure the gunmen to get close, he could use the sack as a makeshift weapon and inflict damage.

Even better, when he opened the sack, two ropes fell out that must have been used to support the tent. He tied up the sack with one rope trapping the stones inside and he tied the branches together with the other rope, creating a missile that he could hurl at the gunmen.

In the campsite to Lincoln's right the

gunmen were calling to each other. He presumed that since their initial search had failed to find him they were now systematically searching the area.

They were sure to look in the gully but, as it was narrow, it would probably be the last place they tried. So Lincoln drew his legs up to his chest and kept quiet, giving himself time to think.

The gunmen's quick return suggested that after the bandits had rowed away they had argued with Stewart and decided to eliminate him. It was also possible that Lincoln's comments had let them work out his and Stewart's identities and that they'd already killed Stewart.

After spending six months hoping he could one day discover his old mentor's fate, this thought made Lincoln chide himself for having ruined Stewart's plans. Then the gunmen's voices sounded close by.

'He must have gone this way,' Kimball said.

'But his only way to escape,' Daniel

said, 'is on the boat.'

'Agreed. So he must be hiding in the undergrowth waiting to flee. I'll try there while you watch the water.'

They'd conducted their debate loudly, making Lincoln smile as he recalled how he and Johnstone had exchanged views in Stein's Pass to misdirect the suspected raiders. He surmised that this exchange meant Daniel and Kimball would act differently from what they'd said. Sure enough, when he heard movement, only one man approached.

Kimball's heavy footfalls stomped to a halt at the base of the slope. This was ten paces away from Lincoln and too far away for him to risk using his makeshift missiles.

For the next five minutes silence reigned, but Lincoln was familiar with the waiting game. If necessary, he could sit here until sundown and take his chances in the darkness; but he didn't need to as Kimball showed he wasn't as confident as he ought to be.

A grunt sounded and Kimball shuffled

from side to side before he loosed off three quick and wild gunshots. Shards kicked from the rockface ten feet above Lincoln's head, but his only reaction was to press his back tightly against the rock.

'Did you get him?' Daniel shouted. Then footfalls sounded as he hurried closer.

'I don't know,' Kimball said, 'but he's up there. Someone's walked over these stones.'

Daniel stopped at the bottom of the slope and Lincoln pictured them staring dubiously upwards, with their hands on their hips. The result of their silent debate came when sustained gunfire ripped out.

The two men splayed round after round into the crack. Lincoln's elevated position meant that even though some slugs sliced into the rock opposite him, they then ricocheted upwards.

The gunfire must have looked impressive and successful to Kimball and Daniel, for when they stopped firing two contented grunts sounded. A whispered debate ensued about who should investigate.

The result came when stones ground against each other as Kimball made his cautious way up the slope. He climbed up the opposite side of the crack so he could see past the corner at the earliest opportunity.

He was sure to shoot indiscriminately when he saw Lincoln and in the confined space Lincoln doubted he could avoid the onslaught. So he raised the bulging sack.

He planned to seize the initiative when Kimball was within five paces of the corner. But it was hard to judge Kimball's progress accurately as every pace Kimball made was accompanied by the sound of dislodged stones cascading down the slope.

Then Kimball cursed and a thud sounded. As stones skidded away, Lincoln pictured Kimball stumbling and falling to his knees.

Lincoln had rehearsed the next move in his mind. In a fluid motion he came to his feet quickly. He swung round the corner, using his momentum to propel the sack.

A moment before he released the sack he saw that he had judged Kimball's position well, but Kimball hadn't fallen over. He was standing crouched over with one hand pressed against the rockface for balance and with a foot raised, as if he'd stubbed his toe.

Kimball didn't register surprise at Lincoln's appearance and even though Lincoln adjusted the sack's trajectory as he released it, Kimball ducked away with ease.

The sack clattered into the rockface above Kimball's right shoulder before rolling to the bottom of the slope. As Daniel moved aside to avoid it, Kimball faced Lincoln, smirking confidently.

Kimball was being slow to take advantage of Lincoln's failure, so Lincoln grabbed his other makeshift missile. He swung back the tied-together branches and launched them at his opponent.

As the branches left Lincoln's hand Kimball raised his gun, but he was only five paces away. By the time he'd taken aim he was too late to avoid the missile. The branches turned end over end once; then, with perfect timing, they jabbed into his throat.

Kimball uttered a strangulated scream. He took stumbling steps backwards and his hands rose to his bruised neck, making him drop his gun. He tried to right himself, but his feet slipped and he toppled over.

Lincoln followed him, scrambling down the slope on his side, controlling his progress by digging his hands and feet into the loose stones. As he passed the position where Kimball had been he scooped up Kimball's dropped six-shooter. Then he jammed his heels into the rocks.

When he came to a skidding halt, his momentum drew him up to a standing position. By now Kimball had slipped to the bottom, from where he looked up the slope to face Lincoln, who now had

Kimball's own gun in his hand.

Lincoln fired, blasting Kimball in the chest and making him drop. Then he looked for Daniel, but the other bandit had fled.

Lincoln hurried down the slope. When he reached the bottom he was moving too quickly to slow down. With his gun thrust out he had careered through the entrance before he could stop to look for Daniel.

His opponent was beating a hasty retreat back to the boat. Within moments he had reached the undergrowth. Lincoln broke into a run and took the same route as he'd used earlier to leave the creek. It kept the sheer rockface to his side to limit the directions from which Daniel could attack him.

As it turned out, he didn't see Daniel again until he reached the water. The bandit had clambered back in the boat, but he hadn't taken the oars. When Lincoln emerged, Daniel levelled his gun on him.

Lincoln went to one knee as Daniel fired, and the shot sliced into the mud a yard from Lincoln's left knee. In retaliation, Lincoln fired back. His slug slammed into the side of the boat before he adjusted his aim and caught Daniel in the ribs with his second shot.

Daniel jerked backwards, his movement making the boat rock, almost overturning it. Lincoln fired again. This time his shot slammed squarely between Daniel's eyes.

Daniel slumped over the side of the boat, making the boat capsize. So Lincoln gained his feet and hurried on.

The going was slow through the mud. When he reached the shallows Daniel and the upturned boat had drifted to the headland. Lincoln considered diving in and rescuing the boat, but the current beyond the headland caught the boat and it speeded up.

Lincoln made his way back to the gully, where Kimball was lying with his head propped up against the rockface while clutching his chest. Bright blood was seeping through his fingers and he didn't react when Lincoln approached, so Lincoln doubted he'd survive.

Even so, he gathered rags from the campsite. He returned and wadded them against Kimball's chest, which made Kimball stir and consider Lincoln through pained eyes.

'Why did you come back for me?' Lincoln said.

'To kill you,' Kimball said, his voice barely audible.

'And Stewart Montague?' Lincoln waited for an answer, but when Kimball said nothing and just closed his eyes, he shook his shoulder and prompted: 'Did you kill Stewart before coming back for me?'

'We'd never kill him.'

Lincoln sighed with relief and shuffled round to sit beside Kimball with the rockface at his back.

'Do you know who I am?' he asked after giving Kimball time to relax.

'You were Stewart's friend,' Kimball murmured, his voice low. 'But you failed him when he needed your help.'

'I suppose I did,' Lincoln said. As he doubted that Kimball would have the strength to answer many questions, he offered some encouragement. 'But I'm pleased you still trust him.'

'Of course I do.' Kimball opened his eyes and considered him. 'Stewart's our new leader. He ordered us to kill you.'

7

'Stop lying about Stewart,' Lincoln muttered, shaking Kimball's shoulder, 'or you won't die peacefully.'

Kimball considered him through glazed eyes. His mouth was slack and dribbling.

'Why would I lie?' he murmured. 'Stewart became Colm's second, and now he leads us.'

Kimball's speech appeared to exhaust him, as his head flopped back against the rock. Then he slid to the side to lie curled up.

Lincoln doubted anyone would use his last words to make up a story, especially since Kimball didn't appear to know that Lincoln was a lawman and that his revelation would give him cause for concern. So he recalled his conversations with Stewart, which he now viewed as being more guarded than they had needed to be.

Worse, Stewart's activities had been consistent with his being a bandit, not a lawman who had infiltrated these men to bring them to justice.

No matter how he looked at it, the man he had trusted the most had dishonoured the badge and sullied the oath of office they had both sworn with pride. So he hunkered down beside Kimball and waited for him to regain enough strength to answer some of his many questions.

As it turned out, Kimball drifted into unconsciousness and Lincoln couldn't rouse him. Later, Kimball's breathing became tortured.

Before sundown, he died.

Lincoln considered working off his irritation with physical exertion and digging a grave, but he didn't reckon Kimball deserved that dignity. So he dragged the body down to the creek and sent Kimball on his way after Daniel.

Then he set about effecting his escape.

Driven on by anger at Stewart's betrayal and the fact that a good deputy had been wrongly arrested at Rocky Creek, he climbed up the slope in the gully. He hoped his frantic desperation to leave would give him the impetus to reach the top. It didn't.

He covered a third of the height before the slope became too steep. The gully narrowed to only four feet wide and running water was slicking the sides. He had to accept that unless he found a long rope, the ascent was impossible.

By the time he admitted defeat, night had fallen. So he built a fire from the remaining firewood and settled down to make his enforced stay here comfortable.

The speed with which Kimball and Daniel had returned to kill him suggested the other bandits planned to return soon. Even if they didn't learn about their companions' fate, they wouldn't expect him to be alive. Since there was only one entrance he could hole up here while the food held out. With only one mouth to feed that would be for at least a week.

With a gun and ammunition, he could fight them off, perhaps even eliminate them before they could land the boat. But as he wanted answers from Stewart before he delivered justice, that thought didn't cheer him and the night was a sleepless one.

First light found Lincoln pacing the site, eager for Stewart to return so he could end the blot on the oath of office they had sworn. But the bandits didn't appear and by noon exhaustion forced Lincoln to sleep.

He chose a spot where he would be hidden from the creek but where he would hear the bandits, if they rowed around the headland.

When he awoke it was dark and, as his situation hadn't changed, he returned to sleep.

The next day he settled into a rhythm of watching and waiting, but that day passed too without anyone appearing, as did the next. The only arrivals of note were the flotsam that washed ashore.

The largest item came from the bridge. It was a twenty-foot-long and two-foot wide post that had holes bored in the sides. He hoped similar items would wash up so he could construct a raft, but by the fifth day that was the only useful item to arrive.

By this time Lincoln had accepted that the bandits had abandoned their hideout and wouldn't be coming for him. As his concern for Haycox's predicament and his hatred of Stewart's actions hadn't lessened, he decided to leave.

He threw debris into the creek and watched its progress. He concluded the safest route was to avoid the headland where the water was choppy, and to head out into midstream.

So at noon he wrapped rope around his chest and tied himself to the post. Then he pushed the post into the creek and slipped into its cold depths, which made him gasp until he became used to the temperature.

He swam using his legs and with his arms resting on the post. As much as he was able, he directed the post towards the upriver headland.

Before he reached it the current hit him. Within moments he was moving downriver faster than he could move forward.

His momentum was still strong enough to take him beyond the headland, and he saw what until now had been out of his view: an area he had tried to imagine during his sojourn. It was as bad as he'd feared.

The high ground continued for as far as he could see. From his low position, it presented a daunting sight, and when he drifted past the headland he entrusted his fate to the vagaries of the creek.

The bandits couldn't have rowed upriver for long, so while the current directed the post, he looked for the place where they had moored the boat.

The surface was choppier than it had been on the day he had been rolled into the water, and every ripple bucked the post, jarring Lincoln's body.

He clung on to the post, judging that holding a floating object gave him his best chance of survival, a theory that became less convincing with every jolt. When the post sailed over a wave that projected it clear of the water, Lincoln banged his cheek on the wood. So he started working on the ropes.

He had tied the knots tightly and the slippery twine was hard to untangle, but after several minutes the rope unravelled, sending him and the post on different trajectories. He was glad he had released himself as, when the post moved out of sight, he saw that the high ground ended 200 yards ahead.

With his head down, Lincoln set off for dry land using strong strokes with his arms and legs, but every time he raised his head for air, he appeared to be no closer to the side. Worse, in the cold water his strength faded fast.

After twenty strokes his legs cramped up. When he tried moving using only his arms, his biceps cramped too.

To alleviate the discomfort he rolled on to his back and used gentle waves of the arms and pushing movements with his legs. This position didn't strain his muscles, so he increased the force he exerted.

When he felt he was making progress he glanced over his shoulder and flinched on seeing that he had moved closer to the side than he'd expected.

A boulder protruded from the water a body's length away while above and behind the boulder the ground rose beyond the extent of his vision. He couldn't tell if he'd moved past the landing point, but he didn't waste time looking as he pedalled round in the water.

He managed to face the rock before he brushed against it. He clawed at the wet and smooth side, failing to stay his progress until he slid free of the rock, only to find that another boulder was twenty yards ahead.

This time the current directed him towards the boulder and he was travelling fast enough to mash him against the rock with bone-jarring speed. He floundered, seeking to find a route that would avoid the impact, but that action somehow constricted his limbs and he didn't move.

Panic clawed at his mind as he feared his strength had failed him, but then rope floated up to the surface and he realized it was still attached to his waist.

With only moments to act before he hit the boulder he dragged a loop of rope out of the water. Finding it was in the form of a noose he launched the rope at the rock.

He couldn't see any projections and he could hurl it only a few feet in the air, so, as he raised his hands before his face, he didn't hold out much hope of success. His hands cushioned the blow and then the swirling current dragged him round the rock.

He could see downriver when he

jerked to a halt, then he slid sideways until his right shoulder slammed into the rock. The rope cut into his waist, but Lincoln didn't mind as the rope had snagged on something.

As waves washed over his stationary form, Lincoln wrapped two hands round the rope and drew himself onward. Water drove into his face, blinding him, and he had to keep turning his head sideways to breathe, but after five tugs the onslaught stopped.

He shook the water from his eyes and saw that he was in a channel in the boulder. Four feet above his head the rope had caught in a crack.

The channel created a calm stretch of water, but Lincoln doubted the rope would hold for long. So he strained his arms and tugged himself up the rope.

The first few movements were hard-fought, but as he drew more of his body from the water, his progress became easier. When he was able to plant his feet on the rock, he surged clear of the creek.

He wasted no time in scrambling upwards and planting a hand in the crack. When he was sure that even if the rope came free he wouldn't slip back into the water, he took stock of his surroundings.

He was perched on the top of an outlying boulder. Upriver there were numerous other boulders that led to the flat area he'd been aiming for.

Downriver the land grew higher and rockier, so it was likely the bandits had gone to the flat area. As it was also likely that this was the only place where he could escape from the creek for some distance, he cautiously sought a route away from it.

On the slippery rocks it took him an hour to reach dry dirt, where he limited himself to a contented sigh before moving on. He found an area a hundred yards from the creek where horses had been corralled.

By the time he was convinced the bandits hadn't returned since they'd left their hideout, Lincoln still hadn't dried out and the cold made the bruises from the battering he'd taken announce themselves.

So when Lincoln set off upriver, he was in the right frame of mind to fight back.

★　★　★

The low sun was blood red and large when Lincoln reached the bridge.

He'd already proved his six-shooter was in working order and the sun had warmed him, but his failure to pick up Stewart's trail hadn't improved his sour mood. So he'd decided to complete his unfinished business at the bridge first.

The workers were milling about as they prepared to end work for the day and he soon picked out Philander Friedman. The overseer was heading towards a group of tents set before the bridge.

With his head down to avoid attracting attention, Lincoln followed. He was fifty yards behind Philander when his quarry slipped into a large tent.

Lincoln speeded up. When he reached the tent he threw back the flap, to be presented with a view of Philander's back as the overseer bent over a desk to study a map of the rail route.

Philander gestured vaguely, signifying he was busy and the intruder should leave, but Lincoln paced up behind him and dug the barrel of his six-shooter into the small of Philander's back.

'I'm back,' Lincoln muttered as Philander tensed.

'I'm pleased you're safe, Lincoln,' Philander said cautiously. 'I wasn't involved in treating you badly.'

'I wasn't just treated badly. Quillon Dee tried to kill me.'

'He was angry. It wasn't his fault the barrel rolled into the creek.'

Lincoln snorted a harsh laugh as he dragged Philander upright. He turned him round and pressed the gun against his chest.

'I thought he'd claim that, but you made a big mistake in claiming it too.

You're now under arrest, as will be everyone who helped Quillon.'

Lincoln tugged Philander towards the exit, but Philander dug in a heel and stood his ground. He considered Lincoln with his eyebrows raised in a show of surprise.

'If you're claiming that shoving you in that barrel was attempted murder, you'll have to arrest every man here.'

'I may do that.' Lincoln grabbed Philander's collar, then he opened his hand, as if he'd had a thought. 'Or I might only arrest Quillon and the ringleaders, if I find out who they are.'

'I haven't got the time to waste on your vendettas. Moulton's commandeered half my men to search for the missing train and I still have deadlines to meet.'

'For all his faults, at least Moulton's helping me,' Lincoln said. Then he dragged Philander out of the tent.

Outside, the workers were still moving off the bridge. Nobody paid them any attention as Philander walked ahead of

Lincoln. He moved stiffly, showing his unwillingness to help. When he tried to veer away past the bridge, Lincoln decided that he should go in another direction.

Lincoln jabbed his gun into Philander's back to turn him towards the bridge. They had reached the area where the tracks would be laid when Lincoln saw the reason for Philander's unwilling steps. Halfway across the bridge, at the point where the topmost layer currently ended, stood Quillon Dee.

Quillon was directing the workers to pass along a line of four men. The workers were scowling as they were frisked and any backchat was met with pushing and muttered threats.

'Quillon keeps everyone in line,' Philander said.

'I've met his sort,' Lincoln said. 'They make more money than the other workers, and for little work.'

'Either way, he's valuable.'

Lincoln snorted with irritation, but Philander now walked with more assurance. The workers trooping by nodded to him, then stopped and glared angrily when they saw that Lincoln was holding him at gunpoint. Before long the pair drew Quillon's attention. He couldn't hide his shock at Lincoln's sudden appearance.

'So you survived,' Quillon called.

'I sure did,' Lincoln said.

Quillon laughed. 'Then it's time I put right that mistake.'

8

Over Philander's shoulder, Lincoln and Quillon glared at each other.

When Lincoln moved his six-shooter to Philander's side to show Quillon he was holding him at gunpoint, Quillon gestured at his men. They faced the advancing Lincoln while the workers picked up on the situation and scurried to the sides of the bridge.

Lincoln noted that Quillon's men had been amongst the group who had shoved him into the barrel. This made clear to Lincoln what his next action should be. Twenty feet from Quillon he stopped and when Philander spotted that Lincoln was no longer holding a gun on him, he seized what might be his only chance for freedom and he leapt aside.

Lincoln let him go and the unexpected ease with which he gained his freedom made Philander stumble. When he dropped to his knees, the nearest of Quillon's men threw his hand to his gun.

Before the man could touch leather, Lincoln jerked up his gun and blasted the gunman through the chest, making him keel over sideways. With the rest of Quillon's men scrambling for their guns, Lincoln fired again while moving to the right.

His second shot slammed into the side of another gunman, making him back into the man standing behind him. This delayed that man's response and gave Lincoln enough time to pound slugs into both men's upper chests, downing them.

Two gunshots tore out from Quillon and the remaining gunman, and they sliced into a post behind Lincoln.

When Lincoln faced them, he saw the reason for their poor aim. The workers had panicked and, being unsure where the best route to safety lay, they were scattering in all directions.

As the chaos blocked his view of the gunmen, Lincoln dropped to one knee to reload. He punched in bullets with calm efficiency.

When the workers thinned out and gave him an uninterrupted view of Quillon and the other man, he snapped his gun up. He fired twice, blasting Quillon in the hip and the other man in the neck.

As Quillon fell to his knees, his gun falling from his hand, Lincoln hurried across the bridge.

Quillon's downed men were so blood-soaked he doubted he'd get any surprises from them. The other workers retreated quickly, leaving only Quillon and Philander.

Philander was wide-eyed and shaking, appearing too terrified to act, while Quillon struggled to make his injured leg work and regain his feet. Then Quillon reached for his dropped gun. His fingers brushed it before Lincoln kicked the gun aside.

'You've got one chance to live,'

Lincoln muttered. 'Tell me about Stewart Montague.'

Quillon glared at him in defiance, but then his other leg gave way and he stumbled, to lie on his side.

'Stewart was a lawman,' he said, his voice strained as he gritted his teeth in pain, 'but he had too much to live for to waste his life on the law.'

'Stewart was the best lawman I ever knew. Something changed him.'

Quillon shrugged. 'The same thing that'll change you, except you won't get a second chance.'

Lincoln had started to ask what Quillon's cryptic comment meant when Quillon betrayed himself with an eye-flick to the right. Such a blatant attempt to distract would never fool Lincoln, but behind him scuffling sounded, followed by a pained grunt.

Lincoln turned and found that he'd gathered help from an unexpected source. His former deputy Richmond Johnstone had arrived and was tussling with Philander.

A knife glinted in Philander's hand. Lincoln aimed at the overseer. Since the two men were entangled he didn't risk firing, but when Philander slashed the knife at Johnstone's face, Johnstone nudged his wrist aside, grabbed his arm and twisted.

As Philander dropped the knife a scrape and a thud sounded behind Lincoln, making him turn back. Quillon was moving for his gun. It was lying four paces away and, in spite of his injured hip, Quillon was struggling to get to his feet.

Quillon tried a different tactic by kicking off with his good leg. With a move that was half a fall and half a leap, he tumbled sideways and his outstretched hand slapped down on the gun.

As he turned the gun in his grip, he looked at Lincoln, who held his fire and shook his head. Quillon ignored the offer to surrender and raised his gun, forcing Lincoln to shoot him for a second time, this time in the side.

Quillon grunted in anguish and rolled on to his back. He tried to get up, but the movement made him roll towards the end of the bridge.

At the last moment he noticed the danger he faced and tried to twist away. With his poor control of his body, the effort had the opposite result and he tipped over the side.

He clawed at the edge, but he failed to secure a grip and dropped from view. A strangulated screech sounded, followed by a splash.

Lincoln checked that Johnstone was controlling Philander, then edged forward. Below he saw only the choppy surface of the water. Then Quillon's inert form appeared, floating face down.

Lincoln watched Quillon until he drifted out of view. Quillon's death irritated him, for it left many unanswered questions. With his head bowed, he headed back across the bridge to Johnstone, who was holding the cowed Philander in a headlock from behind.

'I hope you don't expect praise,' Lincoln said.

'I wouldn't expect it from you,' Johnstone said.

Lincoln nodded and feinted to step aside, but then he jerked back and punched Johnstone's cheek, sending both men reeling away before they fell over.

'In that case,' Lincoln said, 'that won't have disappointed you.'

'I saved your life,' Johnstone said, fingering his jaw.

'You sided with Quillon, turned your back on the badge, and almost got me killed,' Lincoln sneered. 'You got off lightly, not because you helped me but because I've got bigger targets to find.'

With that, Lincoln took hold of Philander's shoulder and dragged him to his feet. He breezed past Johnstone and moved on.

After leaving the bridge he escorted Philander through the throng of workers who were emerging from hiding now that the gunfight had ended. Every worker sneered at him, their anger undiminished by the passage of time, confirming Lincoln hadn't been forgiven.

For now he dealt with his prisoner. But when he reached East Town and headed into the railroad office, Moulton Casement was as surly as the bridge workers had been.

'I've wasted a fruitless week searching for the missing train,' Moulton said, eyeing him with contempt, 'so I'm not in the mood to deal with you coming back.'

Lincoln shoved Philander into the room, letting Moulton see he was a prisoner.

'I had no choice about leaving,' Lincoln said. 'This man tried to have me killed.'

Moulton came out from behind his desk with his expression as incredulous as it had been when Lincoln had arrested Bernie Jacobson.

'Philander had no reason to do that.'

'Then explain why I was shoved in a barrel and rolled into the creek.'

Lincoln watched Moulton's eyes widen with delight before, with a wince, Moulton accepted that the situation was serious. 'While I wait for that explanation, he'll join Bernie in a cell.'

'If that's what happened, he'll answer for his crimes.' Moulton took Philander's arm and moved him on to the jailhouse, but he stopped at the door. 'But he can't join Bernie. I freed him.'

Moulton stayed to see Lincoln firm his jaw with anger before he shepherded Philander inside. With his arms folded, Lincoln sat on the edge of Moulton's desk. Moulton took his time in dealing with his prisoner, which didn't improve Lincoln's disposition.

When Moulton returned Lincoln advanced on him, making Moulton look for a route to his desk that avoided him before he thought better of it and stood his ground.

'Why did you release Bernie?' Lincoln demanded.

'Because he did nothing wrong,' Moulton said levelly. He brushed past

Lincoln and went to the window, from where he stared outside. 'And because I need all the help I can get to find the train.'

'I can provide more help than Bernie ever could.'

'You can't. Men like you do more damage to the law you claim you uphold than the outlaws who break it.' Moulton sighed. 'I got a message to Marshal Yardley in West Town. He's finding out how he can get your badge withdrawn. The bridge should be passable by sundown tomorrow and you'll get your answer then.'

'Why do that?'

'Because after six months you failed to find the bandits, you had no hand in Colm Tobin's demise, the men you killed in Stein's Pass were working men, Bernie is an idiot, and Philander is a good overseer. Quillon Dee is the only wrongdoer you've identified and I bet you've learnt nothing about him. In fact, I'm sure you don't know he was a decent doctor.'

Lincoln had been shaking his head, but this last detail took him aback. To cover his bemusement he joined Moulton at the window.

'Quillon didn't behave like someone who cared for the sick.'

'He's probably hurt more people than he's helped.' Moulton shrugged, acknowledging Lincoln's more conciliatory demeanour. 'But then again, so have you.'

'I don't care what you think about me when you've made the most mistakes.' He pointed at the jailhouse. 'You're holding my deputy.'

Moulton rounded on him with a gleam in his eye that said he'd been looking forward to Lincoln mentioning this.

'Trusting your deputy was your worst mistake.'

'Trusting your fellow lawmen is never a crime.'

'Don't speak so hastily. I assume you'll confirm Deputy Haycox fired the first shot in the Stein's Pass gunfight?'

Moulton waited until Lincoln nodded. 'He didn't shoot at suspected bandits. He fired at Safford Chance, a man who owed him a good deal of money.'

Lincoln shrugged. 'That's not relevant. Haycox was acting as my deputy.'

'He was hiding behind the badge to pursue a personal vendetta, and that's the worst crime of all.'

'If you can prove that, you're right. If you can't, release him.'

'He'll stay where he is until the bridge is finished and I can hand him over to Marshal Yardley.' Moulton smirked with triumph. 'The evidence against him was so overwhelming that he confessed.'

Lincoln winced. Lost for words and lost for an explanation, even to himself, he left the railroad office.

★   ★   ★

Sundown found Lincoln hunched over a coffee. The pungent fumes hadn't cleared his mind, as he couldn't move past the fact that Moulton had been right and that, since coming to East Town, he had conducted his investigation poorly.

He had resisted the urge to seek solace in liquor and he had chosen the Northern Star, a saloon on the opposite side of town to the bridge which, apparently, the bridge workers never visited. Nobody had approached him, so when a man stopped before his table in the corner with a whiskey bottle and two glasses in hand, Lincoln waved him away.

The man didn't move. Lincoln looked up to find that Stewart Montague had come to see him.

'You're taking a risk being seen in public,' Lincoln said.

Stewart shrugged as he sat down. He lined up the glasses and poured them both generous measures.

'I'm not,' Stewart said calmly. 'Nobody knows who I am or what I do. But don't get any ideas. My men are here and if you try anything, this whiskey will be leaking out of a dozen holes.'

Lincoln took the offered drink. While he sipped it he glanced around and confirmed that Stewart had told the truth.

'I don't need a gun to destroy you. One word about who you once were and who I still am will finish you.'

Stewart gulped his whiskey. 'They already know. Before, I was secretive only to save you, not to save myself.'

Lincoln snorted with disbelief. 'Sending men to kill me is an odd way of saving my life.'

'Daniel Tobin and Kimball Sutherland were my biggest rivals to become the new leader.' Stewart smiled. 'I reckoned two armed men would be no match for you and so I used you to help me secure my position.'

'Gloating was never your way. Why are you here?'

'I'm a quicker draw and I have a better aim than you have, but I don't want to have to kill you. So I owe you one attempt to make you give up before it's too late. Luckily, you have a way

118

out, as I've heard the rumour you're finished since clearly your judgement is no longer — '

'My judgement is fine!' Lincoln muttered, gripping his glass tightly. 'I reckoned you were the finest lawman I've ever known and you could be again. It's not too late for you, either. Turn your back on this life.'

Lincoln withdrew Stewart's badge from his pocket, the one he had kept for the last six months, and placed it on the table. When he raised his hand, Stewart planted a finger on the badge and flicked it back at him.

'If you get a new badge, throw them both away.' Stewart filled their glasses. 'That's your only option now.'

'You once told me I should never forget the honour that wearing this badge brings.' Lincoln picked up the badge. 'So I live to bring you to justice, or to make you wear this again.'

'Such choices are irrelevant. Whether we wear a badge or not, we all end up in the same place.'

119

Lincoln sipped his whiskey, nodding as he considered one element of Stewart's recent history.

'Is that what Quillon Dee said when you sought out his services?'

Stewart sighed. When he spoke again his voice was no longer mocking and more like the tone with which Lincoln was familiar.

'I started coughing up blood. I saw a doctor and he told me I had a month, perhaps even a week, to live. So I thought riding with you one last time might cheer me, but the pain was too hard to bear. Bernie told me about Quillon and I was desperate enough to seek him out.'

'As you're still alive, I assume you're pleased that you did?'

'No. Quillon took my money, sold me a sweet drink, and ran. I chased after him, but strangely the pain faded. It made me question everything I believed in, and I decided none of it matters.'

'So you joined the bandits we'd been pursuing?'

'Sure, but then again, to shine the light needs darkness as much as the darkness relishes being banished by the light.'

'I liked you when you spoke sense.' Lincoln laughed and Stewart gave a supportive smile.

'Except I had the sense to use my knowledge of your tactics and procedures to stay ten steps ahead of you. For the last six months you've never got even close to us.'

'I will do now that I know you stole the train.'

'An act that was more memorable than anything I ever did as a lawman.' Stewart leaned forward when Lincoln scowled. 'But as we're being honest with each other: the stolen train was a distraction. While everyone was searching for it, we aimed to get away with the money.'

'The first part of your plan worked, but you're still here.'

'The distraction was my idea, but Colm Tobin was our leader and he decided to leave the money on the train, something

I later made him regret. So find the train and you find the money.'

Lincoln smiled. 'So your bandits aren't as inventive as you claim.'

'Nobody else sees it that way.' Stewart gestured at the saloon with his glass. 'You've been away so you won't have heard. Everyone's talking about the bandits who stole a train, and they all hope we'll get away with it. Nobody will remember your deeds; everyone will remember mine.'

Lincoln gulped down his whiskey and slammed the glass on the table.

'That's nothing to be proud of.'

'I can say the same about you. I know you better than you know yourself and you're no longer fit to be a lawman. You were wrong about the men you shot up, about Deputy Haycox, about me. Worst of all, you were wrong about Richmond Johnstone. He's a good man, a bit like you were when you first rode with me, except you can no longer see that.'

'Johnstone turned on me,' Lincoln snapped.

'And that should tell you everything about your right to wear the badge.' Stewart knocked back his drink and stood up. He pushed the bottle towards Lincoln. 'Drink that. It'll make you think clearly for the first time in a while.'

With that, Stewart turned away. He gathered his men, after which they left the saloon in a furtive way that showed he wasn't as confident about acting openly as he'd claimed. But Lincoln didn't reckon he could do anything about it, as Stewart had been right.

His judgement *had* become poor, and by continuing to act on behalf of the badge, he was dishonouring it as much as Stewart had.

He poured himself a measure and downed it. The fire in his belly made him settle back in his chair and somehow his problems no longer felt so pressing.

He poured another drink, then, to save time, he filled Stewart's glass. Finally he tipped out the dregs from his coffee mug and he filled that too.

9

'I asked you a question,' the angry man demanded. 'Are you Marshal Lincoln Hawk?'

Lincoln had been asked this question several times, but he couldn't summon the energy to raise his head. A muttered oath sounded before someone grabbed his shoulder and tugged him away from his table, sending empty whiskey glasses spinning to the floor.

The room appeared to be swaying, so Lincoln rested a hand on the table to stay upright. He couldn't focus on the men standing before him, but he reckoned there were somewhere between three and nine men.

'I sure don't feel like no lawman no more,' Lincoln said, his speech slurred; then, for some reason he couldn't fathom, he laughed.

Laughing felt good, so he chortled

some more, throwing his head back as he enjoyed the moment. Unfortunately, that tipped him over backwards.

Someone was standing behind him. He stopped Lincoln from falling over although, when he shoved him upright, Lincoln stumbled forward across the saloon room until he bellied up to the bar.

He folded over. The sudden motion made his stomach lurch and nausea burned his throat. A disgusted cry went up, interspersed with laughter as Lincoln vomited over the bar.

The spasms continued until Lincoln reckoned he must have spilled out a whole bottle of whiskey, but that made him thirsty again. He rooted around on the bar until he found a bottle that hadn't been finished yet.

He put the bottle to his lips and upended it, finding it contained only enough whiskey for two gulps. So he threw the bottle at the wall in disgust and, as glass tinkled, he set off down the bar in search of more liquor.

'You got it wrong,' someone said. 'That's no lawman. Look at him.'

'I've seen him before,' the truculent man who had dragged him away from his table said. 'He was shooting up the bridge earlier.'

'That man *was* US Marshal Lincoln Hawk, and he's a formidable lawman. This man's just some drunk who dragged himself out of the gutter so he could crawl into a whiskey bottle.'

'You saying I don't know what I saw?'

A resigned sigh sounded. 'I'm saying your friends got shot up last week and yet again you're looking for someone to blame.'

The truculent man responded in kind, but Lincoln stopped listening to this developing argument as he'd happened upon an almost full whiskey bottle. He gulped a mouthful, then leaned back against the bar with his feet planted wide apart for balance.

Several men were facing off, although as Lincoln was having trouble focusing, he wasn't sure how big the impending fight would be. Then a thud sounded as someone threw a punch. That encouraged other men to throw themselves at each other.

With so much movement going on Lincoln couldn't concentrate on what was happening, although his memory of the numerous other saloon room fights he'd witnessed told him this one wouldn't degenerate into anything serious.

He recalled how once, in what felt like another lifetime, he had stopped such situations. That no longer felt like something he should attempt and when a fighter stumbled into the bar beside him, he wrapped protective arms around the whiskey bottle.

He laughed again as he turned back to the bar, but he kept moving when someone grabbed his shoulder and dragged him away.

'What you laughing about?' that man asked. Lincoln's vision was too blurred to see him.

He waved a dismissive hand at the

saloon room in general, but that only made his opponent grunt in anger and shove him. Lincoln toppled over and landed on his back.

With the whiskey bottle still cradled to his chest, liquor poured over his neck and chin. Lincoln screeched in anguish and rolled on to his side. That made the bottle clatter to the floor and roll away.

With a determined blink, Lincoln willed his eyes to focus on the bottle and he lunged for it. At the first attempt his outstretched fingers wrapped around the bottle and with a deft manoeuvre he righted it.

He breathed a sigh of relief when he saw that only a third of the contents had spilled. So he put his mind to sitting up so that he could enjoy the liquor.

This proved to be harder than he thought it'd be. When he slapped his free hand on the floor and shoved, he slipped back down again.

Legs rocked back and forth around him as blows were traded, so Lincoln concentrated on protecting the bottle until he could work out how to get up.

He had yet to come up with a plan when a face peered at him. It came into focus for a moment letting Lincoln see that Richmond Johnstone had arrived.

Johnstone slipped his hands under Lincoln's armpits and hauled him up from the floor. Lincoln lost his grip of the bottle and whimpered until he found it had become lodged in the crook of his elbow.

'Let's get you out of here,' Johnstone said, 'before someone takes revenge.'

'I'm not going nowhere,' Lincoln said, 'when there's whiskey to be drunk.'

'I've no idea what you're trying to say, so stop talking and just walk.'

'What I said was . . . ' Lincoln said as he was directed across the room, 'was that I'm . . . '

Lincoln closed his eyes as he tried to recall what he had wanted to say, but that made him dizzy. Then he fell over and even when he thought he ought to have hit the floor, he still kept tipping forward.

'So this is the great Marshal Lincoln Hawk,' Johnstone said, his voice seemingly coming from a great distance. 'And to think I once admired him.'

★   ★   ★

Lincoln opened an eye, but harsh light burned deep into his brain so hurriedly he closed it.

He tried to recall recent events, but other than vague memories of being dragged around interspersed with vomiting, he wasn't sure what had happened or where he was.

He tried opening an eye again and this time the light wasn't so painful. He was lying on the floor in a hotel room and Johnstone was moving around near by.

'What time is it?' Lincoln croaked.

'It's long after noon,' Johnstone said, looking down at him, 'and long after the time I started needing your help.'

Lincoln put an elbow on the floor and levered himself up, but that made his stomach lurch. With a groan he settled back down on the floor.

'You, a former deputy who abandoned his duty and turned on me, need my help?'

'Sure, but only after I do this.'

Lincoln started to ask what he meant, but cold water slapped him in the face, making him sit up straight and glare at Johnstone, who was holding an emptied bowl.

Lincoln thanked Johnstone with a curse before he forced himself to his feet and shuffled over to the window. With his hands planted on either side of the window, he looked across the road at the Northern Star.

The sight of broken saloon windows helped him to recall some details of last night's fight, and a twinge of shame hit him with enough force to mask the pounding in his head. He turned to Johnstone.

'Obliged you got me out of there,'

Lincoln said. 'It must have been tempting to leave me.'

'As I said, I can't track down the bandits and the missing train on my own.'

Lincoln found a chair and flopped down into it. A hand supporting his brow, he considered Johnstone.

'And as I said, you stopped having the right to find them when you turned on me.'

'I turned against you, not against the law.' Johnstone glared at him, seemingly defying him to provide the obvious retort, but Lincoln couldn't summon the energy, so Johnstone continued: 'That helped me to learn plenty at the bridge.'

'Go on,' Lincoln said when Johnstone didn't explain.

'Quillon Dee used the bridge for his own nefarious purposes, but he spent too much time on those schemes to be involved with the bandits. Moulton Casement should have known that, except he wound us up to take on Quillon, and I reckon that was a distraction.'

Lincoln nodded, although that made pain slice into his forehead while his stomach churned. He took deep breaths until the discomfort receded, then gave a tense smile.

'I can believe Moulton lied to me.'

'Which means you didn't get everything wrong. The thing you never followed up is why Bernie bothered to follow Colm Tobin's trail to Stein's Pass.'

'That's a fine question. What's the answer?'

'I don't know. Moulton's men Ambrose Taylor and Ingram Watson have led the search along the tracks for the missing train while the rest of his men have laid tracks to the bridge. But Moulton's spent most of his time in Stein's Pass. I couldn't see what he was doing there, but now that you're back we can work together to find out what's interested him out there.'

'You don't give me orders,' Lincoln muttered.

He stood up and walked over to the

bowl that Johnstone had thrown over him. It was empty, but he found water in a jug; he gulped it down into his grateful stomach.

When he'd had his fill he emptied the last of the water over his head and turned to the door. Without comment he left the room and made his way down the corridor with one hand raised to the wall for balance.

Johnstone hurried after him, catching up with him only when Lincoln reached the road.

'So what are your orders?' Johnstone said. When Lincoln didn't reply, he persisted. 'I'm right that you went after the wrong man and you should have investigated Moulton, but it's not too late to rectify that.'

'It is and I'm still thirsty.'

Lincoln turned to the Northern Star across the road, but before he could move off, Johnstone grabbed his arm.

'You're not getting drunk again. We have a job to do.'

'We don't. You turned a gun on me.'

'I've explained that. I disagreed with you and I had to make my disgust look convincing to let me investigate. I didn't know you'd get stuffed into a whiskey barrel.' Johnstone looked skyward. 'Although having seen how you behave, you'd have probably crawled in there on your own.'

'Now that's the first sensible idea you've had.'

Lincoln looked down at his arm until Johnstone removed his hand. Then he set off for the saloon.

As it turned out the owner barred him before he reached the door. When Lincoln turned away, Johnstone was still watching him with his hands on his hips, appearing shocked that Lincoln hadn't forgiven him.

Lincoln ignored him and went in search of a saloon where he might not be recognized. He had to visit three of the other four in town before he found the Lone Eagle, where he could drink in peace.

Sadly, he saw at first hand that

Stewart had been right about the townsfolk's reaction to his bandit gang's activities. The only topic of conversation was the stolen train.

Many of the customers had joined in the search for the train, but their failure to solve the mystery had only excited them more. Everybody enjoyed the audacity of the crime and they were intrigued about how the train had been taken and where it was now.

This only went to sour Lincoln's ill mood even more. The only good thing was that the chatter stopped most people from paying him attention, although some customers still nudged each other while looking at him from the corners of their eyes.

As he had done last night, he picked a corner table where he could avoid unnecessary contact easily. With a whiskey bottle standing in the centre of the table and a glass in hand, he set his jaw firmly, promising that anyone who approached him would regret it.

It was late in the afternoon and the

whiskey had at last defeated his hang-over when Moulton Casement arrived and took the chance.

A muttered conversation ensued at the bar while Moulton and several customers glanced at him. Then Moulton paced across the saloon room with Ambrose and Ingram flanking him, sniggering as they goaded him on to act.

'I heard you were in the Northern Star last night,' Moulton said. He waited for a response, but when Lincoln considered him silently through narrowed eyes he continued. 'Apparently there's no whiskey left.'

'I was celebrating killing Quillon Dee.' Lincoln scraped back his chair and stood up. His uncertain movement rattled the table and he put a hand to it to stay upright. 'Now I can turn my attention on to you.'

Moulton gulped and glanced at his colleagues for support. Then all three men stepped forward.

'You were drunk last night and you're

137

drinking yourself senseless again. You don't have the right to question nobody and come sundown when Marshal Yardley returns, you're finished in East Town.'

Lincoln was prepared to argue that point, but he didn't reply when the men at the bar who had pointed him out to Moulton spread out. Bernie Jacobson was amongst their number.

Lincoln considered Bernie for the first time since he had questioned him in the jailhouse, making Bernie bite his bottom lip nervously and back away to the door.

When Lincoln set off after him with a stumbling gait, Moulton blocked his path. Moulton's gaze was truculent, but Lincoln brushed him aside.

The other two men closed in, forcing Lincoln to stop. He considered them, his eyes rolling, then shoved Ambrose over with a wild flail of the arm that hit the man's shoulder.

With more time to act, Ingram aimed a punch at Lincoln's head, which made

Lincoln sway away. The motion almost unbalanced him, but the moment the blow whistled past his chin, he rocked forward and grabbed his assailant's jacket front.

Lincoln raised Ingram on to tiptoes and threw him at his table, which tipped over, sending Ingram to the floor amidst a shower of whiskey. Lincoln moved on and reached the bar as Bernie slipped outside.

'Hey,' Moulton shouted after him, 'you can't walk away when your whiskey's spilling on the floor.'

The taunt raised a laugh. Lincoln turned to Moulton.

'I'll be back later to finish my drink,' he muttered, pointing a stern finger. 'Make sure you're here. You lied to me and that means you have questions to answer.'

With that, Lincoln stormed out through the door.

10

Bernie was walking purposefully towards the station. This was fine with Lincoln, as this end of town was usually deserted.

After a few minutes Bernie glanced over his shoulder. When he confirmed that Lincoln was pursuing him, albeit with a stumbling gait and on a snaking path, he speeded up to a fast trot while looking around nervously for help.

Nobody was about, so Bernie crossed the road to the station. He was fifty yards ahead of Lincoln when he disappeared from view behind the station house.

Bernie's only option would be to run down the tracks until he fetched up at the end of the line. Lincoln doubted Bernie would have the energy to attempt that, so when he reached the corner of the station house he slowed and sidled round it.

He was right to be cautious, as Bernie was lying in wait. Bernie leapt forward, only to back away at the last moment when he saw that Lincoln had raised his arms ready to grab him.

Lincoln slapped Bernie's cheek, sending him reeling into the wall. Then Lincoln was on him.

He grabbed Bernie's collar and yanked him up to hold him six inches off the platform with his back pressed against the wall.

'The last time we chatted,' Lincoln muttered, breathing acrid whiskey fumes over Bernie's face, making him wince, 'you were telling me about the dead man you found and how his trail led you to the landslide.'

'I told you everything I know about that,' Bernie bleated. 'I did nothing wrong last week at the pass, and I did nothing wrong last year with Marshal Montague. You have to believe me.'

'I will.' Lincoln waited until Bernie's eyes widened with relief. 'But only after we've been through your story from the beginning, starting from the day you first met Quillon Dee. If I don't like any part of your story, this happens.'

Lincoln thudded a low punch into Bernie's stomach, making him gasp out his breath.

'You can't treat me like this,' Bernie murmured when he'd regained his breath.

'I can, and this time Moulton won't save you.'

'Except I will,' Moulton said from behind him before Bernie could reply.

Lincoln hadn't been looking out for anyone following him, but he wasn't surprised that Moulton had caught him up. He dragged Bernie a few inches higher, then swung round to launch him at Moulton.

Bernie clattered to the platform three feet to Moulton's side, but it still made Moulton step away.

With Moulton off balance, Lincoln seized the initiative. He stomped up to him and hammered Moulton's chin backhanded, making his opponent go spinning down on to the platform.

Lincoln stepped forward, intending to deliver more punishment, but heavy footfalls sounded behind him. He turned to find that Ambrose and three of the customers who had been talking about him were coming around the corner.

When seven men had lined up before him, Lincoln looked to the other corner. But that escape route had been closed, as Ingram had taken a detour and was gesturing to other unseen men to join him.

'So it's at least ten men against one,' Lincoln said, glaring at Moulton with bleary eyes. 'You want to wait until more men arrive?'

'I have enough,' Moulton said. 'I refuse to let you continue your investigation in East Town, as innocent people end up dead.'

'Assaulting a US marshal is a serious offence. You're condemning every man who helps you.'

'Enough people know about what you did in Stein's Pass, and they've seen you drinking yourself senseless. Everybody will agree we were right to run a violent drunk out of town and if you ever come back, we'll kill you *before* we stuff your body in a barrel and roll it into the creek.'

Moulton nodded to Ambrose who, along with three other men, advanced on Lincoln while Ingram at the other corner of the station house waited. When Ambrose was three paces away, Moulton sought to gain his feet. Lincoln acted.

Despite his earlier apparent sloth, Lincoln hurried forward. Before Moulton could stand upright he grabbed his right arm. A moment later he'd swung Moulton round to hold him before the advancing men. He drew his six-shooter and jabbed it into Moulton's neck.

'Tell them to back away,' Lincoln muttered in Moulton's ear, 'while you still can.'

'It's a trap,' Bernie said, a comment that made the men on the periphery of the group peel away and seek the safety of the corner of the station house.

Lincoln had expected that a threat to Moulton would make the rest back down, but he hadn't expected them to do so this quickly. When another batch of men decided this was a good time to retreat, leaving only Ambrose and Ingram, Lincoln saw the reason why.

He hadn't worried them, but Richmond Johnstone had. His former deputy was lying on the top of the station house's flat roof with a gun aimed down at the men below.

When Johnstone noted that Lincoln had seen him, he spoke up.

'You men put those hands where I can see them,' he demanded.

Ambrose and Ingram twitched their hands towards their holsters, seeming as if they'd take on the deputy, but Moulton waved a dismissive hand at them. After glaring at Johnstone and Lincoln in turn, the two men backed away.

Johnstone didn't react to their departure and neither did Lincoln, judging it was too late to get answers from them now.

Instead, he settled for shoving Moulton on to the wall and then gathering up Bernie and standing him beside Moulton. By the time Johnstone, having confirmed that all the men had run, had clambered down from the roof, Lincoln was parading back and forth before his prisoners.

'You want to question them?' Lincoln asked.

Johnstone considered his steady gait and even steadier eye with bemusement.

'You sure sobered up quickly,' he said. 'Before, you could hardly walk . . . '

Johnstone trailed off as the obvious explanation hit him, but that didn't stop Lincoln from smiling.

'Last night I had a bad time, but today was different.' Lincoln held his hand out with the palm down and the fingers still to show he was in control. 'I had to make my drunken state look convincing so I could panic Moulton into taking action and proving he has something to hide. Your disgust helped.'

Johnstone winced before, with a smile, he acknowledged that Lincoln had effectively repaid him for his previous actions.

'You fooled me,' Moulton said, 'but I don't know why.'

Lincoln paced by Bernie, looking him up and down before he faced Moulton.

'For one reason: I want to know what you've been doing in Stein's Pass for the last few days.'

'My men were clearing the rail tracks.'

'My deputy saw you out there long after the tracks were clear.'

Lincoln glanced at Johnstone, who nodded as Lincoln acknowledged his status for the first time since his return.

'I'm a railroad man building a railroad.' Moulton spread his hands. 'So I spend time on the railroad.'

'I believe you.' Lincoln waited until Moulton smiled, then he looked at Bernie. 'But Bernie's no railroad man, so he had no reason to be there.'

'He was worried about the landslide.'

'So he told you, except he told me he followed the tracks made by Colm Tobin before his demise at the bottom of a ridge.'

Bernie and Moulton flinched before they turned to each other. Bernie couldn't look Moulton in the eye, which made Moulton snarl before he leapt at him.

As both men clattered to the platform, batting and clawing at each other, Lincoln joined Johnstone.

'I reckon,' Johnstone said, 'that that reaction proves Bernie and Moulton know more than they've let on.'

Lincoln gave both men a chance to work off their anger with frantic blows before he separated them. He grabbed Moulton while Johnstone dealt with Bernie.

Even when they'd been dragged apart the two men lunged at each other, forcing the lawmen to move them further apart. With them unable to inflict damage on each other, Bernie registered how bad this looked and he lowered his fists.

Moulton followed Bernie's lead. When he glanced over his shoulder at Lincoln, his expression was shamefaced.

'Bernie lied to me,' he said. 'I should never have released him.'

'You shouldn't.' Lincoln turned Moulton towards town. 'But I can wait until we're in Stein's Pass to hear why you regret it.'

He waited until Moulton snarled before he pushed him on. Johnstone followed with Bernie held from behind.

On the way into town, the customers who had tried to attack Lincoln had scurried into hiding, but through the saloon windows people watched him leave. Lincoln reckoned everyone would regain their truculence if his hunch that his prisoners would lead him to the missing train didn't pay off.

Fifteen minutes after leaving the station they had secured horses from the stable for the journey and were heading out of town.

Lincoln directed Moulton and Bernie to ride at the front to see how they acted. Aside from casting aggrieved glances at each other, neither man showed outward signs of being annoyed, although when they approached the pass they both slowed, forcing Johnstone to urge them to carry on.

'We looked in the recess and found nothing,' Johnstone said when the two men had moved out of earshot. 'So where do you reckon they'll lead us to first?'

'They'll try to waste our time, so we watch them carefully until they betray themselves.'

Johnstone rode in silence for a while; then he smiled at Lincoln.

'Are you saying you were right all along?'

'I'm saying I was right.' Lincoln returned the smile. 'But so were you.'

Johnstone accepted Lincoln's effective offer of reconciliation with a nod.

'So what do you think happened?'

'The bridge workers we shot up weren't planning to raid the train, but they did hope that by tracing back along Colm Tobin's trail they'd find the stolen money and perhaps even the train itself.'

Johnstone nodded. 'While the bandits did have access to local knowledge, as you thought, except it came from the railroad, not from the bridge. That flow of information let Moulton find out the money was still on the train, so he directed us to Quillon Dee to distract us while he embarked on his own search for the money.'

Lincoln didn't reply as they were now entering the pass. Moulton and Bernie had reached the recess ahead of them. The two men rode by without looking that way, but their rigid postures suggested the location concerned them.

Lincoln and Johnstone speeded up. Catching them up, Lincoln stopped them with a narrow-eyed look. All four men dismounted.

'As you organized most of the town to search for the missing train every-where except for Stein's Pass,' Lincoln said, 'it'd seem that to find it I only have to watch where you don't look and then look there.'

'At least I won't have to listen to that kind of nonsense for long,' Moulton blustered. 'In a few hours Marshal Yardley will be able to get across the bridge and once I explain to him how you've treated me, you're finished.'

'Unless I find the train first,' Lincoln said.

Moulton folded his arms with a determined gesture that said he'd regained his former composure, but Bernie gulped and glanced down the pass before he acknowledged he'd betrayed himself by lowering his head and staring at his boots.

Johnstone laughed, confirming he'd seen Bernie's reaction, and Lincoln looked along the pass. Aside from the hollow created by the original landslide, the rockface was smooth. Lincoln directed them to move on to the hollow.

The workers who had cleared away the mound had shoved the debris to the opposite side of the tracks. Standing facing the hollow, Lincoln could see that further landslides were likely as stones were slipping free and rolling to the bottom.

Loose rocks were scattered over the revealed area and the rockface itself had slipped down so that the strata formed a chevron. The area being fragile, exploring would be dangerous; perhaps that was the reason why everyone had been cautious, but what they were looking for, Lincoln couldn't see.

He was about to turn to Johnstone to ask his opinion when he noticed a dark area at the top of the pass. He edged forward with his eyes narrowed, a movement that made Bernie and Moulton shuffle from side to side.

With his confidence growing that he'd found something important, Lincoln moved until he could discern the dark area, seeing it was a space that opened up between two rocks.

Light couldn't penetrate for far enough to illuminate what was in the space, but as he didn't fancy clambering up there, Lincoln turned to

Moulton and raised an eyebrow.

'That's where you've been exploring,' he said. 'Quit with the lies and tell me what's behind that opening.'

Moulton tipped back his hat, seemingly weighing up the benefits of co-operating. Then he shook his head and gave a confident smirk. Bernie, however, uttered a resigned sigh and then spoke up.

'It's not an opening,' he said. 'It's what's left of a cave entrance after the bandits collapsed it.'

'Why was it collapsed?' Lincoln said, although there could be only one answer.

'To hide the train.' Bernie gestured at the space. 'When Colm Tobin stole the train, he buried it in there!'

11

Only when Lincoln peered into the hole and saw the top of a train car below did he believe Bernie's story.

He stood back to let Johnstone look down while he considered the lie of the land. From higher up the improbable final location of the missing train seemed less unlikely than he'd first thought.

A cave had once been here, but a rockfall had blocked the entrance. Some of those rocks had slipped away and they had created the mound that had stopped the train.

Only from high up could he see marks on the ground, which led away from the tracks and which implied that a length of rail had been laid temporarily to take the train into the cave. When Johnstone moved back, he pointed them out to him. Both men faced Moulton, who sighed before he responded.

'The cave was once used for storage,' he said. 'It looks like that's how it's being used again.'

Lincoln and Johnstone narrowed their eyes and even Bernie looked skyward at Moulton's poor attempt to appear innocent.

'If this cave was so well known,' Lincoln said in a sarcastic tone, 'I'm surprised you didn't search here earlier.'

Wisely Moulton didn't reply, and Lincoln directed him to head into the hole first. Bernie followed, with the lawmen bringing up the rear.

Sufficient light filtered through the hole to let them see the path downwards, which was as steep as the route up to the hole.

The last few paces down were treacherous and Moulton slipped creating a cascade of rocks that took the rest of them with him. Moulton and Bernie went sprawling on their chests on the top of the car in an ungainly fashion, while the lawmen managed to leap down.

Lincoln explored the available space, finding provisions and a lamp. The excavations that had been carried out had uncovered only this one car, while the heap of rocks ahead was big enough to suggest the rest of the train was buried here.

Johnstone kicked dust aside, then knelt to tap the wood.

'Have you found a way down into the car yet?' he asked.

Moulton got to his feet. He looked away as he apparently tried to maintain the impression that he knew nothing about this situation, but Bernie shrugged.

'I've not been down here,' he said. 'I've only looked through the hole.'

Moulton muttered to himself, but he said nothing else. When it became clear he wouldn't take the opportunity to explain himself, Johnstone spoke up.

'So what do we do now?' he asked.

'I made sure Ambrose, Ingram and

the others saw us leave town,' Lincoln said. 'They'll be here soon and we'll be waiting for them.'

★　★　★

At sundown, Lincoln was lying in the opening peering down the pass.

Johnstone was looking towards East Town. Below, Bernie and Moulton were clearing the car roof, although they were following Lincoln's orders as slowly as they could get away with.

With the cave lit up, Lincoln could see the extent of the excavations. He judged it would have taken several days to burrow down to the top of the car. As the space where Bernie and Moulton could throw rocks was limited, Lincoln doubted they could free even the endmost car, but he hoped that if they cleared enough space to reach a window he could explore inside.

'I gather you no longer have a problem with me,' Johnstone said, breaking into Lincoln's pondering.

'I don't,' Lincoln said with a smile, 'and I gather you no longer have a problem with me.'

When Johnstone nodded, Lincoln checked that the other two men weren't paying them any attention. Even so he shuffled closer and, in a lowered voice, he told Johnstone what had happened since the incident at the bridge the previous week.

When Lincoln revealed the identity of the new bandit leader, Johnstone stared at him in shock before bunching his fists. His troubled posture registered that he understood why Lincoln had been so annoyed since he'd returned.

'A lawman who goes bad deserves to suffer,' Johnstone said after a while.

'A lawman who goes bad deserves a second chance to remember the honour of the badge.' Lincoln waited until Johnstone gave a dubious nod, then he continued: 'I intend to give Stewart the ultimatum that he'll wear the badge again or I'll kill him.'

Johnstone opened his mouth to reply,

but then he looked along the pass. A few moments later hoof-beats sounded as riders approached down the tracks.

Seven men were arriving, but in the gloom Lincoln struggled to discern who was coming until the lead rider was below him. Then he snarled with irritation.

'I assume from your reaction,' Johnstone said, 'that you know these men?'

'It'd seem Moulton's men aren't as inquisitive as I expected.' Lincoln pointed. 'That's Stewart Montague, and he looks confident. So we lie low and pick our moment to act.'

Lincoln directed Johnstone to head down into the cave, to dim the light and to keep Bernie and Moulton quiet. When Johnstone returned, Stewart and the bandits had dismounted in front of the hollow, confirming that they knew what was inside.

Stewart ordered men to guard both directions along the pass while he ordered others to work at the base of the hollow. He didn't look upwards, suggesting he was unaware of the high entrance.

Lincoln couldn't discern what they were doing, but the rising moon had yet to light the pass when someone lit a brand, which showed that the bandits were burrowing into the rocks carefully. As the area was unstable, Lincoln nodded as he solved the last element of the mystery.

Colm Tobin's body had been dirty and that meant, despite Stewart's claim, that his injuries hadn't come from a fall but from being crushed. He had been digging into the cave when there'd been a landslide and he'd become trapped.

Lincoln would probably never find out whether Stewart had caused the landslide, but afterwards he had dragged Colm's body out and dumped it elsewhere. But then, with the mound of dirt arousing the curiosity of Bernie and Moulton, individually, Stewart had been forced to hole up until their interest had faded.

Now Stewart had returned to claim

the money, but before Lincoln could congratulate himself on piecing together the bigger picture, Johnstone got his attention and pointed at the man who was clutching the brand. When Lincoln saw what had concerned him, he winced.

'Is planting six sticks of dynamite,' Johnstone said, 'our moment to act?'

Lincoln raised his gun before thinking better of starting a gunfight. He had lowered it when light flared below as the man lit the fuse to the dynamite, that had been crammed into a crevice at the bottom of the hollow.

In short order the bandits scurried away. The speed with which everyone moved made Lincoln doubt whether he and Johnstone had enough time to escape to the relative safety of the pass.

So he patted Johnstone's arm and, with only the glow from the lamp below to light his way, he went in the opposite direction. Johnstone was at his heels as both men slid down the slope in a cascade of stones that made Moulton look up with anger after he and Bernie had cleared the roof.

Bernie wasn't visible, but Lincoln's warning gestures silenced Moulton's complaints, although Moulton couldn't translate Lincoln's gesture to get under cover and he merely stared at him.

Lincoln landed on the roof and pitched forward. Then, on the run, he jumped down into the hollow that Bernie and Moulton had created beside the car. When he saw that the top half of a window was clear, he leapt for it.

'Follow me,' he said simply as he slipped inside, 'or die.'

Johnstone followed Lincoln and a moment later clattering sounded as Moulton scampered after him.

In the poor light Lincoln couldn't see if Bernie had already taken refuge in the car, neither could he see where the most sheltered position would be. Rocks had spilled in through the windows, but the middle of the car was clear, so he sat in the centre.

Johnstone joined him and the two men hunched over. When Moulton scrambled inside, he sat beneath the window with his knees drawn up to his chest.

He placed the lamp beside him and shot them an odd glance that demanded to know what was happening. Lincoln didn't reckon that knowing would help him, so he pressed his hands over his ears.

A muffled thud sounded, the noise not as loud as Lincoln had feared. He glanced at Johnstone, who shrugged, but the hope that the dynamite had been ineffectual fled when crunches sounded on the roof of the car.

The noise was a prelude to a barrage of rocks slamming down on the roof. The motion rocked the car, knocking the lamp over and extinguishing the light, although as Lincoln could still see he assumed that the cave entrance had been opened up.

The creaking of wood above made Lincoln look up, expecting that a rock would break through, but the roof held firm. Presently the noise level reduced.

When the dust settled Johnstone gestured around the car.

'Where's Bernie?' he said with a significant glare at Moulton that made him look away.

Moulton didn't reply, but raised voices sounded near by, so Lincoln resisted the urge to follow up his deputy's demand. When the voices came closer and he heard Stewart Montague issuing orders, he drew his gun and crawled along to lie beneath the window.

The blast had made most of the rocks that had filled the cave spread out into the pass, freeing the end cars. But to his relief the bandits moved past the car without investigating inside.

Clearly they were unaware that the car was occupied: they had no reason to suppose it was. Even so, while Stewart explored deeper in the cave, Lincoln and Johnstone stood on either side of the door and Moulton stayed in the shadows.

After fifteen minutes the bandits

hadn't returned, and Lincoln assumed they had found a route into the recesses of the cave and that it was there that the money had been buried.

Presently, scrambling sounded near by. Lincoln got Johnstone's attention and when the door rattled, both men tensed.

Johnstone would see the newcomer first. The moment the door edged open for a crack he leapt forward and grabbed the arm that was coming into view.

Johnstone yanked the newcomer forward and Lincoln trained his gun on him, but when the man went to his knees in a stream of moonlight cast through a window, he held his fire.

Bernie had returned and slung over a shoulder was a laden saddle-bag.

'Where have you been?' Lincoln demanded.

'I found a gap through the rocks,' Bernie said with a shrug as he hefted the saddle-bag. 'Then I came across the money.'

Lincoln and Johnstone both shook their heads and even Moulton snorted with derision, but before Lincoln could question Bernie, approaching footfalls sounded. The lawmen adopted their former positions on either side of the door while Bernie and Moulton crawled across the floor to sit beneath the windows.

'There has to be a way through the rock,' a man said on Lincoln's side.

'We need to clear the cave,' Stewart Montague said from the other side. 'Get these cars out of the way.'

The sound of Stewart's voice made Lincoln clench a fist, but he and everyone else in the car stayed silent. For the next thirty minutes the men moved around outside, as the car was uncoupled and horses were hitched up to it.

Presently the car moved with a lurch, making the loose stones crash around inside and forcing everyone to jerk around as they dodged the shifting heaps. Once the car was moving freely, the stones settled at the back and, when the light level increased, Lincoln stood beside a window.

Johnstone stood on the other side of the car and both men peered outside as the car slipped through the entrance and then on into the pass. Lincoln couldn't see Stewart as the bandits busied themselves with uncoupling the horses so they could drag the second car outside.

'When do we act?' Johnstone asked when they'd been left alone.

'I want Stewart,' Lincoln said. 'He's the leader and if we take him, the rest will fall apart.'

'Agreed. But we're outnumbered and these two will only hinder us. We shouldn't risk everything on a plan to make him wear the badge again.'

Lincoln didn't agree, but he acknowledged his deputy's point with a nod. Although when the bandits again emerged from the cave entrance without Stewart, he had to admit he might have to put aside his intention and seize any opportunity that came their way.

The bandits struggled to drag the second car outside and the horses strained for some time before, in a rush that was followed by thuds and a dust cloud, the car surged out of the entrance. This time Stewart followed it and, as the car was dragged towards them, he beckoned urgently for the men to return.

These men uncoupled the horses and, as they scurried back to the cave, gunfire tore out. Lincoln peered through the window, but he couldn't see where it had come from.

As Stewart took refuge in the cave entrance, the other bandits joined him, leaving the second car to roll along until it crunched into Lincoln's car, making both cars clang into the rail tracks. The impact made Lincoln's car roll backwards.

After the car stopped, it rolled forward until it lodged against the back of the second car, its motion suggesting that some or perhaps all of the wheels had settled on the rail tracks.

In the cave entrance Stewart organized his men to take up positions at both sides while others found rocks to hide behind. They all looked up, so Lincoln examined the top of the pass.

Although he saw movement, the light was too poor to pick out individual men. But when Moulton chuckled, Lincoln didn't need to guess who the new arrivals were.

Ambrose and Ingram had taken the bait at last, and they had come out to Stein's Pass to claim the money for themselves.

12

'How many of your men will be out there?' Lincoln asked.

'Enough to do what you never could and eliminate the bandits,' Moulton said with a wink that showed he was no longer concerned about being honest about his plans.

As if to confirm his claim, gunfire pounded at the cave entrance pinning the bandits down. The moment the first volley ended a second volley started up, making one bandit lose patience and stand up.

He fired twice before three gunshots to the chest cut him down making him tip over sideways. Lincoln judged that this time the gunfire had come from the side and the bandits also figured out that they were being attacked from ground level, as they retreated into the cave.

Within a minute forms moved through the shadows and settled down on either side of the cave. Both groups glanced at the top of the pass suggesting they were awaiting the order to attack.

'Do we step in?' Johnstone asked.

'Let them settle this,' Lincoln said. 'We'll arrest the survivors.'

'I'm pleased you've accepted you can't help Stewart.'

'I didn't say that. Stewart will defeat Moulton's men.'

The taunt made Moulton shake his head.

'We'll find out soon enough,' he said.

Although the gunmen couldn't have heard him, the men on either side of the entrance filed inside to disappear into the darkness. While covering gunfire blasted down from the top of the pass, a new burst of gunfire broke out in the cave.

In the small space the gunfire echoed and made it sound as if dozens of men were fighting for their lives. The outlines of running men appeared in the entrance, their darting movements showing that a frantic and confusing battle was raging.

Faced with superior numbers and an inferior position, Stewart and three men burst out from the entrance. They skirted around rocks while keeping in the shadows.

At first they weren't fired upon, which allowed them to reach the second car before Moulton's men realized who they were and splattered lead at them.

This gunfire kept them pinned down and, when other men appeared in the cave entrance and fired at them, Lincoln concluded that these four men were the only survivors of the onslaught.

'Time to step in yet?' Johnstone asked.

Lincoln slapped Johnstone's back and he moved to the door.

'Give me time to talk to Stewart,' he said. 'Then we end this.'

When Johnstone nodded, Lincoln slipped through the door. He was in the dark, but moonlight lit up the other side of the car while the shooting rattled on beyond his sight.

When he peered over the rail he saw that the car was sitting on the rails while the back corner of the second car, which was at right angles to his car, had nudged up against it. As there was a slope through the pass and then down to the bridge, Lincoln surmised that without the second car, it might roll away.

He jumped down and made his way along the side of the second car. He couldn't see any movement in the pass and he reached the end without trouble.

He glanced round the corner and confirmed the bandits had hunkered down along the front of the car where they'd trained their guns on the cave entrance. Their senses must have been attuned for surprises as one man turned to Lincoln before he moved out of view.

So before he lost the element of surprise completely, Lincoln hurried on. With rapid gunfire he shot the nearest man through the chest, down-ing him, and shot the second man in the side, toppling him over backwards.

Then he turned his gun on the third man, but this man was Stewart and he'd already aimed a gun at Lincoln's chest. Worse, the fourth man wasn't visible.

'Did you organize this ambush?' Stewart said when Lincoln raised his gun skywards.

'No. It's Moulton Casement, and his men are better organized than yours are. But you didn't shoot me and that confirms you still want a better future. Wear the badge again and together we can end this.'

'Accept I'll never do that,' Stewart laughed. 'I haven't fired, but that's not to spare you.'

A footfall sounded behind Lincoln, alerting him to the presence of the fourth bandit. He swung round as that man stepped forward with a knife in his hand. He slashed at Lincoln's back.

While twisting Lincoln stepped aside

and the knife whistled by only inches from his right arm. His assailant's momentum made him stumble until he fell forwards at full length. Lincoln heard scrambling as Stewart came round a heap of stones piled against the back wheel.

Stewart skidded, making the stones spread out as he disappeared round the corner. On that side of the car Stewart moved through moonlight and accordingly gunfire blasted from the cave.

Lincoln turned back to the other bandit, who shuffled along on his knees and looked up to meet Lincoln's raised boot. The kick sent him rocking backwards so that his head clipped the back of the car.

The blow made the man glare at the car with irritation. Lincoln saw the reason for his surprise when the car loomed over him and he realized that it was rolling forwards.

Lincoln backed away, which gave his opponent enough room to get up and flee, but on the stony ground the man struggled to gain purchase. Lincoln added to his problems by stepping up behind him and hitting the back of his neck two-handed.

The man went down and rolled out of sight. A strangulated scream sounded, which was cut off with a sickening crunch.

When Lincoln saw that the man had fallen in the path of an advancing wheel he followed Stewart. As the car shuddered to a halt, he gave the corner a wide berth and, with his head down, he hurried on.

Behind him gunshots hammered into the car. He ran on to the first car where he slipped into the shadows and hunkered down.

He couldn't see Stewart; worse, in a disorientating moment the moon emerged from behind the car and illuminated him, encouraging Moulton's men to fire. Slugs sliced into the ground around him and he leapt back into the shadows where he worked out what had happened.

The car was moving, not the moon. Freed of the obstacle, it was now rolling down the tracks, although only at a snail's pace.

Lincoln couldn't see anybody through the windows so he clambered on to the back and then charged in through the door. Moonlight now lit up the inside of the car, where Johnstone and the others were kneeling on the floor with their hands on their heads.

Lincoln turned round to find that Stewart was standing behind the door. He was holding the others at gunpoint.

'I guess,' Stewart said, 'it was always going to end this way.'

Lincoln considered Stewart's gun and then his own gun.

'I still hope,' Lincoln said, 'you'll return to the light without encouragement.'

Stewart laughed. 'I believe I'm in charge here.'

The creaking of the wheels grew in volume, confirming that the car was still trundling along the rail tracks and that they'd speeded up. When Lincoln glanced through a window, the other car was no longer visible, although he couldn't see the sides of the pass well enough to judge how fast they were moving or how far they'd go.

'Moulton is my prisoner, but his men have decimated your bandits and they'll come for us before we can inch forward much further. Join me and we can take them on.'

'It's a tempting offer.' Stewart pointed at the saddle-bag that Bernie had thrown aside. 'But what that bag offers is more tempting.'

'Everyone gets tempted sometimes, but I know you. You'll lower that gun and help me take on the men who want the money.'

Bernie and Moulton both muttered under their breath that this was unlikely, and even Johnstone shook his head.

'Listen to your deputy. I've devoted too much time to this robbery to leave without the money.'

'You won't leave this car.' Lincoln raised his gun a mite for emphasis. 'You will defend it though, as a lawman.'

The two men considered each other. Reflected light let Lincoln see Stewart's eyes and they were as stern as were his own.

Before either man was forced into making a tough decision, shouting sounded outside. When Lincoln glanced through the window he saw movement. Moulton's men were now pursuing the moving car.

The wheels were rattling, so the car had speeded up and they were now passing the recess where Lincoln's problems had started. That meant they were a hundred yards from the end of the pass, where the ground was more open and an ambush would be easier to mount.

They were also travelling at a walking pace so the men could clamber on board easily at a time of their choosing.

'I'll defend myself,' Stewart said, 'and I'll leave when I see an opening.'

'Try anything and I'll kill you.'

Stewart smiled, seemingly pleased to have goaded Lincoln into that response. He turned his gun on Lincoln.

'If you try anything, *I'll* kill *you*.'

Lincoln had tired of trading threats and so he backed away to get a better view through the windows. Behind the car, riders were slipping through the moonlight, cautiously sizing up the situation.

'How far,' he asked, 'will we roll before we stop?'

His question hadn't been directed at anyone, but Bernie spoke up, his nervous tone confirming he was being truthful.

'We won't stop,' he said. 'The slope carries on to the bridge.'

'Except,' Moulton said, speaking up for the first time in a while, 'the tracks haven't reached the bridge yet. So we'll roll off the end of the line. Then we'll crash.'

'But only if,' Bernie whined, 'your men don't get to us first.'

Moulton nodded, appearing in control despite the situation, but Lincoln directed a triumphant glare at Stewart.

'And so we wait for you to join me.' Lincoln pictured the distance to the bridge, the likely speed they'd reach and then halved the time he thought they had left. 'I reckon you've got ten minutes to put on the badge before we crash.'

'And if I don't?' Stewart asked.

'We'll stand here until we die.'

Stewart looked to the roof, shaking his head, but when he looked down it was to face Lincoln jerking his gun up to shoulder height to aim at his chest. Lincoln smiled as Stewart's failure to react with instant gunfire confirmed his belief that he didn't want to shoot his old friend.

'I won't just stand here and meekly let Moulton's men get on board and kill us.'

Stewart glanced at his own gun, which he'd aimed at Lincoln's stomach. The battle lines being drawn, Lincoln retreated into a corner where he could watch Stewart while not being seen from outside.

He didn't object when Stewart picked his way around a heap of stones to stand in the opposite corner. As both men directed their anger at each other, the other men got to their feet.

Stewart had disarmed Johnstone and thrown his gun up against the wall. Wisely Johnstone didn't force an end to the confrontation by trying to reach it; instead he moved to a window.

'We're out of the pass,' he reported. He peered down the tracks. 'The riders are spreading out, but Ambrose and Ingram are making them stay back, as if they expect trouble.'

He looked at Lincoln, but Lincoln said nothing, so it was left to Bernie to respond. He stood between them facing the door.

'You two,' he said, 'can sort this out after we've beaten them.'

Lincoln and Stewart shook their heads as did the other two men, albeit for different reasons. Bernie grunted in irritation and walked down the car to the other door, where he peered through the inset window.

He didn't look perturbed, so Lincoln assumed that the following men hadn't made their move yet. He couldn't blame them, as the lack of response from the car would have disconcerted them, but he didn't reckon that would hold them back for much longer.

Now they'd moved out of the pass he could see the ground clearly and they'd speeded up to a man's running pace. This made it increasingly hard for the men to get on board, and the riders hurried on to draw alongside.

Men peered through the windows on either side, but they didn't appear to see anyone as nobody looked at any spot for long. Then they rode past the car.

Ambrose shouted an order. Then a thud sounded and Ingram shouted from the other side of Lincoln's corner. The frantic tones made Lincoln think the first attempt to clamber on board had failed.

For the next ten minutes he heard no more orders. Then two distinct crunches sounded, giving the impression that Ambrose and Ingram had leapt on board.

In the car everyone cast nervous glances at each other before turning to Lincoln, who shook his head.

'We do nothing,' he whispered, 'until Stewart wears the badge. I've kept it for six months and now is the moment he takes it back.'

He removed Stewart's badge from his pocket and tossed it to Stewart, who in a reflex action caught it. Lincoln smiled and Stewart returned it thinly, acknowledging Lincoln's small victory before he held the badge out at arm's length.

'The moment I drop this,' Stewart whispered, 'I'll fight back.'

'You won't drop it. You're a lawman. Act as one.'

Shuffling sounded behind the door, so Stewart didn't reply. The movements were clearly made by Ambrose and Ingram standing on either side of the door and picking their moment to act.

This development encouraged Moulton and Bernie to seek cover behind heaps of stones. So Lincoln directed Johnstone to stand side-on to Stewart so that if Stewart shot him, he'd struggle to kill him too, but Johnstone stayed where he was and raised a hand.

A moment later the rattle of the wheels changed pitch, suggesting they'd reached a steeper part of the tracks. Then the car lurched as it speeded up, but this wasn't what had concerned Johnstone as the door at the opposite end flew open and two gunmen burst in.

They both sidestepped, seeking the corners, which gave Johnstone enough time to react. He hurried down the car towards the right-hand man while Bernie took on the man on the left.

In the fast-moving car the gunmen struggled to keep their balance, but the other men had become used to the rhythm; they reached their targets before either of the intruders could raise his gun.

Johnstone grabbed his opponent's gun hand and thrust it high while jabbing a punch into his ribs.

Bernie wasn't so sensible; with his head down he slammed his shoulders into his opponent's stomach, making him fold over as he backed into the wall.

Both men went down as Johnstone and his opponent strained for control of the gun, making Stewart edge forward.

'Your deputy's fighting for his life,' he said, 'and yet still you do nothing.'

'My deputy's winning,' Lincoln said, 'but I'll still do nothing until you wear the badge.'

Stewart shook his head and removed two fingers from the badge, showing he was about to drop it, but before he could open his hand, the gunmen outside acted.

Ambrose kicked open the door and burst in brandishing his gun, while Ingram stopped in the doorway.

Ambrose considered the two pairs of fighting men, then nodded at Moulton who, with a weary expression, pointed, making Ambrose turn to face Lincoln. Seeing Ambrose's confusion, Ingram came in and stared at Stewart in surprise.

For long moments Lincoln and

Stewart kept their guns aimed at each other while Ambrose and Ingram looked from one man to the other as they tried to understand the situation.

The impasse couldn't last for long and Lincoln reckoned that the moment he was threatened Stewart would turn on Ambrose. Lincoln resolved that if he kept the badge, he'd let him live, but he didn't get to test his resolve as a high-pitched screech started up at the side of the car.

The sound grew in volume and pitch. Then the car lurched to the right.

'End of the line,' Moulton said. 'Now we crash.'

13

A second screech sounded, giving Lincoln the impression that the other set of wheels had become detached from the tracks, making the car jig around and throwing him into the wall.

All concerns about his stand-off with Stewart fled from his thoughts as he faced the problem of escaping from a car that would crash within moments.

As he struggled to right himself, Stewart fell over while the other men jerked from side to side, but then the stones scattered over the floor went sliding along. They slammed into the open door with sufficient force to close it and then tear it away from the doorjamb.

The shifting stones and grit made purchase on the floor impossible, so Lincoln slid along until he lurched into the doorway. He put hands to either side and held on until Ambrose slammed into his side as he too lost his footing, tearing Lincoln's hands away.

Entangled, both men careered outside. Ambrose slapped Lincoln's back as he tried to push him over the front, but Lincoln thrust out his hands and stilled himself against the rails.

Lincoln came to a sudden halt, making Ambrose stumble, so Lincoln jabbed a sharp shoulder into his chest, which knocked him aside. While Ambrose struggled for balance, an unfortunate bump bucked the car, making him fold over the rail and disappear from view.

Lincoln took stock of the situation. In the moonlight the ground appeared to be rushing towards him while fleeing bridge workers peeled away to avoid the speeding car.

The car had left the tracks, but the wheels must have found purchase on the hard ground and they were slowing as they moved through the workers' camp. The exhilaration of the cold night air and his unexpected survival made

Lincoln throw back his head and laugh.

His laughter died after a single snort. Fifty yards ahead was the bridge and they were rolling towards a point a hundred yards upriver where in the moonlight the glittering crests of the waves looked like jagged glass.

Lincoln reckoned the car would roll on into the water, so he turned, planning to leap off the side. But Ingram was standing in the doorway with his gun thrust out. With the car lurching around he couldn't keep the gun steady, and when he fired the slug clinked against a rail a foot away from Lincoln's side.

Ingram took more careful aim and a gunshot blasted, but Ingram hadn't fired. He staggered forward while doubling over, his free hand rising to his back. He had been shot, presumably, by Stewart.

Lincoln grabbed Ingram's shoulders and threw him over the rail. As Ingram tumbled into the path of the speeding car, they reached the top of the riverbank. Then they tipped over the edge.

The car ploughed down the slope towards the creek, its wheels no longer turning as they cut furrows through the soft ground. Despite the slight slope, Lincoln felt as if he was looking down into the water, so he pushed against the rail to avoid tipping over into the path of the car.

Halfway down the bank the car slewed to the left, tearing Lincoln away from the rail. With a desperate twist of the body he turned the motion into a lunge for the doorway.

His hand closed on the door jamb and his momentum veered him into the car. Then the car tipped over.

He tumbled, hit the floor on his side, then slid towards the wall. A moment later the car sliced down into the water, sending him tumbling back the other way.

He flailed with his arms, seeking to grab hold of something to still his motion. He grabbed a fleeting hold of

Johnstone's arm before he was dragged away. Unable to control his movements he fetched up against a wall, although with the car tipping over he couldn't tell if it was a wall or the roof or the floor.

From all sides water cascaded down, drenching him and sending him scooting sideways on his back. His experience of the previous week in the barrel helped him to stay calm. While he could still breathe he drew in air and he resolved not to act decisively until he could orient himself.

The water sluiced down so quickly that he struggled to keep his eyes open, but he continued to move until he thudded into a corner. He planted a hand on each wall to hold himself steady as the water poured in through the windows and the car rocked.

His head averted from the strongest stream of water, he looked around. Although it was too dark to see anyone, he could see that the roaring water was filling the car.

When a wave of water rose above him, he used the purchase he'd gathered on the walls to lever himself to his knees; this still didn't get his head above water, so he struggled to his feet.

When he stood up the water reached his chest, but the force of the incoming water wasn't as ferocious as before; now he could stand without holding on to the walls.

Lincoln took a deep breath and worked his way along the wall to the nearest window. He managed to draw in another breath before he moved into the water that was surging inside.

He grabbed the sill and shoved his head forward, but the force of the water was still too strong for him to get outside. So he walked his hands up the side of the window and tried to sit on the sill.

He still didn't move and it wasn't until he felt tightness in his thigh that he realized someone had grabbed him. He swirled round and through the deluge he faced Moulton, who was glaring at him, his eyes blazing with fury.

With an angry grunt Lincoln planted a heavy hand over Moulton's face. With his back braced against the wall he shoved, sending Moulton tumbling away into the swirling water.

Moulton slipped below the surface. Lincoln waited for him to emerge, but when the water reached his neck he turned to the window.

Within moments the water rose above his head, but that meant not much more water could come inside, and with Moulton not hindering him he was able to clamber on to the sill easily.

Using one hand to grip the wall, he slipped outside and raised the other hand to the roof. Then he patted around for something with which to draw himself up.

He felt the smooth, rounded edge of the roof and his hand was cold, as if it had emerged from the water, giving him hope that the car was floating on the surface. He swept his hand along the edge, then flinched when it snagged on something.

He tried to move his hand but it was trapped, although when the constriction moved down to his wrist, he realized that someone was on the roof and was trying to help him. He locked hands with his unseen helper and kicked off from the sill.

The man on the roof tugged and in a surge Lincoln came out of the water and flopped forward, so that his arms and upper body lay on the roof. When he was sure he wouldn't slide back into the water, he gathered his strength and rolled over on to his side.

He scrambled away from the edge to lie in the middle of the roof. Above him the dark underside of the bridge was passing overhead.

When the car moved beyond the bridge he heard shouting. Men were peering over the side of the bridge. As it was unlikely they would be able to help, he turned to the man who had drawn him out of the water.

Lincoln winced. His helper was Stewart.

Worse, Stewart was dry and he still had his gun, while Lincoln had lost his six-shooter during the confusion of the crash. Lincoln sat upright and Stewart matched his action by sitting so that the two men faced each other down the length of the roof.

To either side the water lapped against the edge of the roof, but the car appeared to have settled in the water and was floating downriver at a steady rate.

'Obliged you saved my life,' Lincoln said with forced good humour. He could see that the roof was unoccupied except for them. 'Where are the rest?'

'Only we two survived.' Stewart reached behind him and dumped the saddle-bag on the roof. 'Along with this.'

Lincoln sneered and moved to the edge. The water was above the windows, so anyone who was inside the car would be under water now.

He judged that with numerous windows and two doors, more people than just himself and Stewart should have been able to get out, so he looked upriver. The water was too choppy for him to see anyone, but as he searched a worrying idea hit him, making him swirl round.

Stewart's grim smile acknowledged he'd understood the situation.

'You killed the others,' Lincoln muttered.

'Getting out first had its advantages.' Stewart mimed taking pot shots at targets in the water. Then he showed Lincoln his empty hand. 'And I did it after throwing away the badge.'

'Then you threw away your last chance to make amends, and I'll have to arrest you.'

Stewart laughed. 'I knew I was right to save you. Who else could amuse me like you do?'

'There's nothing amusing about men dying over a saddle-bag full of dollars.' Lincoln got to his feet. 'And the worst thing about this is: you know that.'

Lincoln walked down the car. When that forced Stewart to get to his feet and back away, Lincoln speeded up, growing in confidence that, despite the threats they had traded, Stewart wouldn't kill him.

He was five feet from Stewart and thrusting out a hand for the saddle-bag when Stewart stopped moving. He looked Lincoln in the eye. Then he fired.

As pain lanced down his right arm, Lincoln turned away, twisting. Bent double, he held his wrist and warmth dribbled down his forearm, but when he found he could move the arm, he concluded that Stewart hadn't shot to kill him.

He turned back to Stewart, and Stewart's confident smirk confirmed his intent.

'That shot,' Stewart said, 'was to show you that you don't understand me.'

'I do understand you. You didn't kill me.'

'Except that when this car fetches up, I will. Then I'll leave your body on the roof as a warning to other lawmen who might pursue me.'

'They won't heed you. You'll be hunted down and destroyed.'

'I stole a train.' Stewart gestured at the car. 'I sailed the train downriver and escaped. I'll be remembered. Nobody will remember the lawman who died pursuing me.'

'Decent folk will . . . ' Lincoln trailed off. He had intended to goad Stewart into firing as a last defiant act, but someone was moving at the other end of the car. He avoided attracting Stewart's attention by glancing at the night sky. 'Why do you need to be remembered?'

'You're changing the subject. Now I know you have a plan.' Stewart shrugged. 'But nobody lives for ever.'

Lincoln adopted a position that let him see the man holding on to the edge of the roof.

Lincoln couldn't see who had survived, but he'd rested an arm on the roof while keeping his head beneath the edge. His casual posture suggested he hadn't heard them talking and he wasn't aware that anyone else had survived.

He wondered if Stewart had admitted to the return of the illness that had changed him, but he also figured that discussing this might make him agitated and notice the man who was hanging on to the roof. So he relaxed his posture and kept his gaze lively to give the impression he was waiting for an opportunity to act.

In response, Stewart watched him intently. To hold his attention Lincoln prodded his injured arm. He could flex it and he found a painful spot from a nick.

Reassured, he sat silently as the car drifted downriver. When the clouds covered the moon the lower light level made the riverbanks appear as dark smudges against the night sky. Then a large headland came into view ahead.

Stewart's belief that they would wash up appeared likely. The third passenger must have reached the same conclusion, for he raised himself to get on to the roof, letting Lincoln see that the survivor was Deputy Johnstone.

Lincoln coughed to cover any sound the deputy might make; Johnstone caught on to the problem they faced, for he paused and then moved on silently.

'You reckon we'll wash up somewhere before sunup?' Lincoln asked as a distraction.

'You know where we'll end up.'

Lincoln nodded. 'Flotsam from the bridge beached at your haven.'

'It did, but even more of it ended up further downriver, which I assume is where you escaped to.'

Lincoln smiled because Johnstone had clambered on to the roof, and because Stewart's escape attempt could fail through bad luck if they were to land earlier than Stewart expected.

'I did, but you have to hope we don't get trapped in your hideout as I ate all the food and I barely got out of there alive.'

Stewart glanced at the riverbank to his left with apparent concern. Lincoln judged the bank was closer than the last time he'd looked and the dark form of the headland was looming ever nearer.

Lincoln got to his feet and spread his arms wide apart so that Stewart didn't glimpse Johnstone from the corner of his eye. This gesture only made Stewart sneer. Then he raised his gun.

14

Stewart's apparent change of heart bemused Lincoln until he saw that Stewart was looking past him.

Lincoln turned to look over his shoulder and found that Johnstone wasn't the only one to have survived the crash. Bernie was trying to clamber aboard and, unlike Johnstone, he wasn't being quiet.

Bernie rolled on to the top of the car and flopped down into a pool of spreading water. Then he wriggled and slapped his arms as he struggled to warm up.

'Where have you been hiding?' Stewart demanded.

Bernie glanced at him without fear, indicating that he was just pleased to have survived.

'Air trapped down there,' Bernie murmured in a manner that suggested he was suffering from shock. 'Been struggling to keep my head above water.'

He cast bemused glances at the other men on the roof. Lincoln, having sized up the changed situation, checked on Johnstone's progress.

The deputy was sneaking up on Stewart using careful paces. Behind him a headland was only twenty lengths of the car away.

Despite the dark, Lincoln recognized the entrance to Stewart's hideout. It looked as if they'd beach at the spot where Lincoln had found the post he'd used for a makeshift raft.

Johnstone noticed where Lincoln was looking and he glanced at the nearest headland. When he turned back he met Lincoln's eye, confirming they'd take their chances within moments.

Several people were now on the roof; Stewart was sure to get a grasp of the situation before long, so Lincoln wasn't surprised when Stewart gave Bernie an odd look. Then Stewart swirled round to follow Bernie's gaze.

He faced Johnstone, who was five paces away. Johnstone reacted by moving to advance on Stewart, but Stewart thrust out his gun arm, making him slide to a halt.

Lincoln jerked forward, only for Stewart to swing his arm round in an arc and pick him out while backing away.

'So now I have to decide,' Stewart said with a confident smile, 'which one of you dies first.'

Lincoln and Johnstone glanced at each other as they sought to co-ordinate their attack, but Bernie reacted first.

'We're going to crash,' he shouted, his desperate cry loud enough to make Stewart look to where the car was heading.

Stewart's mouth opened wide, suggesting that he hadn't realized how close they were to beaching. Then he went to one knee, which proved to be a wise precaution as scraping sounded beneath the car a moment before the car jerked.

The movement knocked Lincoln over and made him slide sideways on the slippery surface. He dug in a heel, but he couldn't stop himself and the next he knew he was tipping over the edge of the roof.

Cold water slapped him in the face before he sliced down into the inky darkness. He fought to right himself and within moments he bobbed back up to the surface.

When he emerged the car loomed above him as it floated by and he couldn't see the three men who had been on the roof. Then gunfire erupted and someone shouted in anguish.

Lincoln slapped his uninjured arm against the side of the car, but it was moving quickly and he couldn't find purchase. So he swam one-armed alongside it, heading towards land.

After the first burst of gunfire no further shots sounded, giving him hope that Johnstone and Bernie hadn't been harmed. When his feet touched land, he stood up and waded out on to the muddy foreshore, where he turned back to the car, which was standing side-on to him as it ploughed through the shallows.

He was too close to see anyone on the roof, so he backed away, but after a few paces cloying mud coated his boots and he ground to a halt. He fought to move on, but it took him a minute to take five steps, so he sought the easiest route away along the edge of the water.

When he reached a patch of relatively solid ground he stopped and sized up the car, which was shuddering to a halt with the front turned towards him. Its momentum had driven half of the car out of the creek and water was pouring through the windows, but he still couldn't see anybody on the roof.

He edged from side to side while craning his neck, but in the poor light the roof appeared deserted. He looked at the water and, as if Stewart had been waiting for that moment, his adversary loomed up from the roof.

He leapt off the front with his arms

thrust forward. Lincoln only had enough time to raise a forearm in front of his face before Stewart crashed down on his chest.

Stewart's momentum sent both men tumbling over. Lincoln landed on his back on the soft ground, with Stewart bearing down on him.

Lincoln squirmed, but he succeeded only in burrowing down into the mud. Water filled in around him. With an injured arm and the ground being slippery, he couldn't get enough traction to buck Stewart, but thankfully Stewart had the same problem and couldn't gather a tight hold of him.

Lincoln kicked out, dislodging his opponent and making him fall to the side. Then Lincoln sought to right himself. To the accompaniment of splashing and sucking noises, he got to his knees.

He faced Stewart, who was also kneeling and was as drenched as Lincoln was. Water dripped from his body and, when Stewart threw a punch at his face, a clod of mud came loose and splashed on Lincoln's chin, while the fist passed by his shoulder.

Half-blinded by the mud, Lincoln directed a punch at Stewart, but his matted clothing made him struggle to raise his fist and the blow whirled through the air, pausing short of Stewart's face.

With a grunt of irritation Lincoln rocked back on his haunches and gained his feet. Then he wasted no time in turning and heading for drier land.

Slurping noises and curses sounded behind him as Stewart followed, but Lincoln concentrated on being the first to reach a point where he could stand his ground. After ten slow paces, Lincoln put his foot down on ground that didn't give way. In delight he turned.

Stewart was hunched over and swaying as he struggled to make progress, but when he registered that Lincoln was making a stand, he stopped to consider him.

'I assume,' he said, 'you've finally

stopped trying to make me become a lawman again?'

'Never,' Lincoln said.

'You should. The money is on the car roof and I shot the other two.'

Lincoln narrowed his eyes. 'That changes everything. Now you'll die, as all lawmen killers do.'

'I'm pleased we can stop taunting each other and end this.'

Stewart withdrew his gun from his pocket. He wiped it clean while watching Lincoln, his teeth gleaming with confidence in the night.

Lincoln reckoned he could slip into the darkness and elude capture for a while, but the moon emerged from behind low clouds and bathed the area in light, banishing those plans.

The undergrowth was a dozen paces to his right and the intervening land was glistening and soggy-looking. To his left stood a collection of boulders, but they were at the water's edge and he'd only enjoy their cover by ducking beneath the surface.

The sheer headland being twenty paces behind him, he stood tall and faced Stewart.

'So end this,' he said.

Stewart shrugged. 'Only when you make your move.'

'I have no plan.'

'Now I know you're planning something, and I know every ruse you might try.'

'You do know me, except I know you and you can't kill a friend in cold blood. I have to threaten you, and I'm not.'

Lincoln turned his back on Stewart. Then with steady paces he walked towards the rockface.

'Don't turn your back on me,' Stewart shouted after him. 'You don't deserve to die with a bullet in the back.'

'Why should you care?' Lincoln said. He stopped in the shadows in front of the rock.

He considered the crumbling rockface. He'd deemed it impossible to climb the last time he'd been here and the moonlight didn't illuminate the rockface well enough to see anything other than loose ledges.

He turned to face the advancing Stewart, while backing away until his shoulders rested against the rock. Then he slipped his uninjured arm behind his back.

While he felt around for loose rock, Stewart stopped and laughed.

'Thank you for making this easier for me. You deserve to die facing your foe while trying a hopeless plan.'

'I have no plan other than — '

Lincoln broke off when Stewart jerked his gun arm up to shoulder height, the suddenness of his movement leaving Lincoln in no doubt he'd fire. So Lincoln swept his hand around until a rock moved when he tugged on it.

As Stewart fired, Lincoln dropped to one knee, the motion tearing the rock free. Slithers of stone cut into his cheek and it was several heartbeats before Lincoln realized that Stewart had hit the rockface above his descending shoulder.

Lincoln keeled over on to his side. He hoped that in the low light Stewart wouldn't notice the result of his poor aim and he lay still with his eyes half-closed and the rock clutched in his right hand.

For a while Stewart considered him. Then he moved closer with his gun still thrust out.

Stewart kicked him in the ribs. When that made Lincoln roll over on to his back and he didn't react, Stewart grunted in triumph and knelt down.

'As I told you,' he gloated, 'I know your ruses, and trying to find a weapon wasn't worthy of you.'

Stewart uttered a sigh of relief, then backed away while rising. Before the opportunity was lost Lincoln jerked his right hand up swiftly and hurled the rock.

Lincoln had aimed for Stewart's temple, but with Stewart getting up, the jagged rock caught him beneath the jawline.

Lincoln leapt to his feet and moved to wrest the gun from Stewart's grip, but Stewart fell over. By the time Lincoln was standing over him, he saw he'd inflicted more damage than he'd expected.

The sharp rock had sliced into Stewart's jugular and his life blood was pouring out on to the damp ground.

Lincoln planted a firm foot on Stewart's gun hand.

'You may have thought you knew all my ruses,' he said, 'but twenty years ago you saved my life before I got to use that one.'

'You were always more sneaky than I was,' Stewart murmured.

'And you were always more decent than I was. At the last your aim was poor and I reckon that's because you couldn't bring yourself to kill me.'

Stewart clamped his lips shut, suggesting he wasn't prepared to give him the satisfaction of confirming whether this was true, but his eyes flickered with acceptance that he'd been beaten. Then his head flopped to the side.

Lincoln watched the former marshal

in case he was trying a ruse of his own.

When Stewart's gurgling breath quietened he stood in silent vigil over his dead friend, trying but failing to recall the last good time they'd enjoyed together.

Then he walked away, turning his thoughts to reclaiming the money from the roof. Before he reached the water's edge, a more pressing matter grabbed his attention.

A body had washed up and the clawed marks in the mud showed he was still conscious.

Lincoln hurried over to him. When he knelt beside the body, he realized that his deputy had washed up.

Lincoln turned him over and Johnstone rolled on to his back with a hand clutched to his chest. The fingers were dark with fresh blood.

'Is that you, Lincoln?' Johnstone murmured, keeping his eyes closed.

'It is,' Lincoln said. 'We defeated Stewart and we have the money. Everything will be fine now.'

'I'm pleased we completed the mission.' Johnstone breathed deeply; pain contorted his face. 'And that I'll get to die a lawman.'

15

Sunup found Johnstone in better spirits than he had been in last night now that he was lying beside a warming fire while wearing dry clothes. When Lincoln investigated his wound in the daylight, it wasn't as bad as they'd both feared.

The bullet appeared to have lodged against a lower rib. Lincoln reckoned that provided he kept the wound clean and he got help to Johnstone quickly, he would have a fighting chance. So Lincoln put his efforts into their escape and what he found soon improved his spirits too.

Bernie had survived as well and, despite Stewart's claim, he was unharmed.

He was sitting huddled up on a boulder at the water's edge. He'd claimed the money and it was in the saddle-bag at his feet, but the realization that there was no easy way out of the hideout made him surrender without a fight.

With Bernie's help Lincoln examined the beached car. They found Moulton's drowned body along with the two gunmen who had got on board before it had crashed.

He tasked Bernie with removing the bodies. By the time he'd lined them up on land Lincoln had collected enough timber from the car to construct a better raft than he'd been forced to use last time.

While Bernie searched for soft earth to bury the bodies, Lincoln lashed wood together. When Bernie returned to report he'd clawed out shallow graves, the raft was already taking shape.

'Dig one grave away from the other three,' Lincoln said when he'd inspected Bernie's work.

'Why?' Bernie asked.

Lincoln didn't reply, but, sitting by the fire, Johnstone took an interest in proceedings. He pushed himself to his feet and made his slow way towards them.

'Stewart Montague was once a lawman,' he said. 'Lincoln wants him treated differently.'

Bernie looked doubtful, so Lincoln grabbed his shoulder and swung him round to face him.

'It's obvious why I want him buried separately,' Lincoln said. 'Stewart Montague died as a lawman.'

Bernie's mouth dropped open in surprise, but when Lincoln glared at him he looked to Johnstone for support.

'You can't say that,' Johnstone said.

'Stewart wanted to be remembered after he died, and he will be. We'll make sure everyone knows he was working under cover to undermine the bandit gang and because of his bravery they were defeated and the money was reclaimed.'

Johnstone shook his head. 'The law is about the truth. There's no truth in that.'

Lincoln smiled and went over to Stewart's body. He rummaged in his pocket until he recovered Stewart's badge.

'If that's the case, why didn't he throw this away?' Lincoln paused to give Johnstone time to shrug before he continued. 'He kept it because he never abandoned his duty.'

'How can I believe that?' Johnstone spread his hands, an action that made him wince and clutch his side. 'You could have found it and planted it there.'

'You have my word as a lawman that I didn't.' Lincoln returned to Bernie, where he grabbed his collar and hoisted him up on to tiptoes. 'And you have Bernie's word too, provided he wants to stay out of jail.'

Bernie nodded eagerly, but Johnstone sighed.

'I understand why you're saying this, but it's wrong. I want to continue being a lawman and I can't live a lie.'

'You have to, for the honour of the badge and for the sake of every lawman who wears it. They have to believe that

men like Stewart Montague don't aban-
don their duty or none of this makes
sense.' Lincoln tossed the badge to
Johnstone. 'I can live with it. Can you?'

Johnstone hefted the badge on his
palm. Then with his free hand clutched
to his ribs, he shuffled over to Stewart's
body. He dropped down to his knees
heavily and pinned the badge on his
jacket.

'Get Marshal Stewart Montague
buried, Bernie,' he said. 'Then we can
get out of here.'

Johnstone struggled to get back to
his feet. Then, with a shuffling gait, he
walked back to the fire. He didn't meet
Lincoln's eye, but Lincoln could live
with it too, for the badge.

THE END

Other titles in the
Linford Western Library:

DARROW'S GAMBLE

Gillian F. Taylor

'Set a thief to catch a thief!' It's a risky strategy for a lawman to take, but Sheriff Darrow has very personal reasons for wanting to catch bank robber Tom Croucher. Forced to stay in Wyoming, Darrow is relying on two convicted criminals, Tomcat Billy and Irish, to do the job for him. But Tomcat hates Darrow, while Irish wants to go straight. They join Croucher's gang, but who deserves their loyalty — the outlaw or the sheriff?